# SINCE YOU'VE BEEN GONE

# SINCE YOU'VE BEEN GONE

Mary Jennifer Payne

Editor: Shannon Whibbs
Design: Colleen Wormald
Printer: Webcom

Cover design: Laura Boyle
Cover image: © youngvet/iStockphoto.com

**Library and Archives Canada Cataloguing in Publication**

**Payne, Mary Jennifer, author**
Since you've been gone / Mary Jennifer Payne.

Issued in print and electronic formats.

ISBN 978-1-4597-2818-9 (pbk.).--ISBN 978-1-4597-2819-6 (pdf).--
ISBN 978-1-4597-2820-2 (epub)
I. Title.

PS8631.A9543S55 2015 C813'.6 C2014-902140-2 C2014-902141-0

1 2 3 4 5 19 18 17 16 15

We acknowledge the support of the **Canada Council for the Arts** and the **Ontario Arts Council** for our publishing program. We also acknowledge the financial support of the **Government of Canada** through the **Canada Book Fund** and **Livres Canada Books**, and the **Government of Ontario** through the **Ontario Book Publishing Tax Credit** and the **Ontario Media Development Corporation**.



Printed and bound in Canada.

Visit us at
Dundurn.com | @dundurnpress | Facebook.com/dundurnpress | Pinterest.com/Dundurnpress

Dundurn
3 Church Street, Suite 500
Toronto, ON
M5E 1M2

*To my parents, Susan and Dennis,*
*for their love and support*

*In memory of Tyson Bailey, and all the other young men of Regent Park and Lewisham, whose lives were taken too soon due to violence*

*A big thank you to the Toronto Arts Council for their generous support in completing this novel*

# CHAPTER 1

Today I punched Ranice James in the face. My fist connected with her cheekbone and she dropped to the asbestos-filled tiles of our gymnasium floor like a bag of marbles. Now I'm officially suspended. I might even be expelled. According to our principal, Mr. White, Safe Schools will be involved for sure, and maybe even the police. The police. Just the thought of the police being involved in any way makes me want to dry heave all over my bed.

Mom is going to be so disappointed. She won't "kill me," which is what other kids say when they make a major life mistake like having a party while their parents are away for the weekend, or smoking weed, or getting caught shoplifting. My mom doesn't get angry. Ever. She won't even raise her voice at me. Anger is something she avoids like a bad dentist; I guess she figures we've dealt with enough of it in this lifetime. But I think it's natural. Anger, I mean. It's a natural emotion. And it would be so much easier to deal with her getting angry like normal parents. Instead, she'll be disappointed … and worried. More than anything, my suspension is going to make her super anxious because there will be follow-up meetings about it at school. And at these meetings there will be questions. Questions about our situation at home and what might be making me so angry. I wonder if Ranice's mom will want to press assault charges. I doubt it. Most people in our neighbourhood have a pretty uneasy relationship with the police.

I walk over to the window, press my hands against the windowsill, and let my forehead rest against the cold glass. The streetlamp in front of our townhouse is already on; its yellow light illuminating the spiderweb-shaped cracks in the windshield of the abandoned car at the curb and the dirty snowbanks left over from last week's blizzard.

I look at my watch. It's nearly six o'clock. Mom should be home by now.

We have this pact, this unspoken rule, that if one of us is going to be late, no matter what the reason, we have to call. And we can't just leave a message; we need to speak to the other person. That way we can be sure we're both safe.

I try to push down the nervous, sick feeling that starts to spread in my stomach.

*She's fine. She'll be home any minute.*

Sensing a chance to get petted, my cat Peaches jumps up beside me and stretches out along the windowsill. Her throaty purr vibrates against the palm of my hand.

The ringing of my phone startles both of us. Peaches leaps off the windowsill as I run over to my bed to grab it. I glance at the screen and smile. It's Mom.

"Hey," I say. "Where are you?"

"Edie. You need to pack. I'll be home within fifteen."

I feel like I'm in an elevator that's plummeting thirty stories to the ground.

"What?"

I don't know why I'm asking; we've been through this so many times.

My mother's breathing is heavy, frantic.

"Just two suitcases and not too heavy. Janice will be with me. Look for her car. It's the grey Toyota."

"I know what she drives," I snap.

Mom ignores that. "And Edie, don't open the door for anyone. No matter what."

As if I'm that stupid, I think. Anger is rising in me like hot lava. It's not her fault. I know that. Mom didn't ask for this any more than I did. But I'm angry anyway.

"What about Peaches's carrier? Is it still in the basement?"

There's a pause.

"Mom?"

"I'm so sorry, Edie." Her voice is strangled with emotion. "But we can't take her this time."

The blood drains from my body. Peaches meows softly from the bed where she's curled up, anxiously watching me. It's like she understands what we're talking about.

"What do you mean?" I shout. "You can't do this. Why can't we take her?"

"We'll talk when I get there," she says. "I need to go. We don't have much time."

Then there's the familiar click of our call ending and I am left staring for the last time at my bedroom, at Peaches, at the bed I'll never sleep in again. And suddenly my suspension doesn't matter at all.

## CHAPTER 2

My life is never stable. It's as if I live balanced on a series of tectonic plates like the ones under the Pacific Ring of Fire. We learned about tectonic plates last year in our Grade 9 geography class during a unit on earthquakes. I hated our teacher, Mr. Chahil, this round ball of a man with a head as smooth as a balloon and a disgusting habit of checking out female students' boobs during class, but I was fascinated by thought of these plates underneath us, just waiting to screw around with our lives and turn everything upside down.

I could totally relate. My life will seem secure for a while, but if you watch long enough, it eventually shifts, just like those plates, and everything I'm used to changes again. The frustrating thing is that each time my life changes, I leave little pieces of myself behind. Sometimes it's a photograph or a gift I really liked or even just a project I did at school that I was really proud of. More often, it's a best friend, a supportive teacher, or a boy I'm crushing on. I was ten years old when we began running, and I've been leaving pieces of myself, of my heart, in different apartments, cities, and schools ever since.

This time it's much worse.

My first day in England, the sky outside the bedroom window is so dark and grey I actually forget for a few moments that it's afternoon. It seems so much more like early morning. You know, that time just around dawn when everything is kind of hazy as though you're seeing thc world through a thin layer of smoke.

Mom is sitting perched on the edge of the bed. I can feel the mattress sinking in her direction. She's rubbing my back. This is something she's done to comfort me as long as I can remember.

"Edie? Are you awake?"

I open one eye and attempt to nod at her. My entire body feels as though it's filled with cement bags. I've never felt so exhausted.

"Wake up, sweetheart," she says, giving my shoulder a gentle shake.

"Mwamf," I reply, burying myself face down into the pillow. My breath reeks. I can't remember if I even brushed my teeth before going to sleep.

Then I begin to remember. I'm not at home in my bed. And I'm not in Regent Park.

The first thing that hits me is how musty this new place smells, like a grandmother who'd been living with five cats and a closet full of mothballs.

I sit up and swat Mom's hand away because now I remember everything.

I rub my eyes. The skin beneath my lids feels gritty.

"What time is it?"

Mom glances at her wristwatch. "I forgot to change this," she says, her voice strained. "It's 10:00 a.m. in Toronto. I guess that makes it ... three o'clock here."

Here. So it isn't a bad dream. This time we're not even in Canada, let alone Toronto. I think about last night's plane ride during which I tried to hide my tears from my mother and the stupid stewardess who kept smiling at me in that fake way they reserve for children. I'd spent most of the flight with my blue British Airways blanket pulled up, leaning my cheek against the cold of the tiny window, watching the clouds and lightning swirl below us.

"We're in London, Edie," Mom whispers. "The city I grew up in."

I don't reply. Instead I let my gaze wander around the room. Rivulets of water slide down the windowpane. It's pouring rain outside. Yesterday in Toronto the weather was freezing cold with a wind chill that would make tears freeze to your cheeks. The way winters should be.

"I know where we are," I say flatly.

It's not Mom's fault we're here. But I'm angry all the same.

"What did you do with Peaches?" I ask. Mom made me wait in the car with Janice while she took care of last-minute things and locked up the house.

"Edie," Mom begins, her voice low. "We talked about this last night."

"What did you do with my cat?"

"We couldn't bring her. We just couldn't. There wasn't time."

"I know all of that. But what did you do with her?" I'm shouting now but I don't care. Tears tickle my cheeks.

Mom doesn't answer. She just stares down at her hands. They're folded on her lap like limp fish. I hate that she's so calm, that she doesn't tell me off for yelling at her. It makes her seem weak.

"Who's taking care of her? Is Janice?" I'm in her face now.

"I did the best I could. She was left out with plenty of food and water."

Peaches. My beautiful cat Peaches. Despite everything, we'd managed to keep her with us for four years. She must be so terrified and confused. We always kept her inside and now she'd been abandoned and left to fend for herself in the middle of winter in Regent Park. I glare at my mother.

"I hate you," I hiss. "I hate you and I hate this shitty life."

I throw myself back down on the bed and toss the thin comforter over my head.

"I'm so sorry," Mom says. The mattress recoils as she stands up. And just before the door clicks shut, I hear her choke back a sob.

# CHAPTER 3

The first day at a new school is always the worst. And this time is no different. I'm standing around on the grey asphalt of the schoolyard, trying not to notice all the students walking past me without so much as a glance. I feel invisible. A group of girls huddle beside me, discussing their weekends.

"God, aren't you lucky! My mum dragged me to stay with her new boyfriend at his flat in Reading. His feet smelled like rotten cheese every morning and I couldn't eat breakfast because I felt sick. I don't know why she wouldn't just let me stay at home."

"Really, France is not all *that*. Would've rather stayed here. After all, they just speak French in France so I couldn't understand anything on the telly."

I hate this part the most. The part when I'm walking around completely alone, checking my phone twenty times a minute, trying to look like I'm waiting for someone, trying to think about anything other than the fact that I look like the biggest loser on earth.

Fitting in at this school will be a million times harder. I'm a new kid: a kid from a different country. I have a different accent. I don't know what's cool when it comes to clothing and hair. And of course there's always the issue of my name. God only knows what Mom was thinking when she named me. I asked her once, and she told me she thought Edie was a beautiful name for a girl. That's when I knew she inhaled. I just hope she didn't do it when she was pregnant with me.

I stumble over an uneven patch in the asphalt. Stupid shoes. When Mom registered me at the school, they gave her an "emergency" second-hand uniform. The uniform fits well enough, thank god, but my black flat shoes were one of the things I had to leave behind in Toronto. Shoes and boots make suitcases heavy. So now I'm here, trying to walk as normally as possible in a pair of my mother's black ballet-style flats, which isn't easy because her feet are a full size larger than mine.

I stuff my hands farther into the front pockets of my jean jacket. I don't understand why I'm finding it so much harder this time. After all, it isn't like I haven't experienced all of this before. The bell will ring soon, which will make it easier because then I can just blend into my classes.

"Oi! Watch your head!"

I feel the soccer ball whiz past my right cheek

before I really know what's happening. A couple of centimetres closer and it would've slammed into the side of my face like a speeding train. God, then people would notice me!

A boy with crazy Afro hair dashes past me. The ball is rolling quickly out the school gates and toward the street, which is jammed with cars crawling bumper to bumper like a colony of determined ants. I watch as he belly flops on top of the ball at the last second, then scrambles to his feet and holds it over his head like a trophy.

"Hurry up, Rodney! You wanker!" another player shouts from across the yard. I look over at the group of boys standing around, impatiently waiting for the ball so they can continue their game.

One of them catches my attention right away. Maybe England isn't going to be as bad as I think especially if there are more guys this cute here. Amazing smile, stylishly messy blond hair … he's a bit taller than the rest of his friends, too, and looks confident in a good way. I like boys who are confident. Most guys my age are either blabbering idiots or act super aggressive, all gangsta and up in your face with their pants down around their knees. And he's wearing glasses. I know it's stereotyping, but I think the glasses make him look intelligent and thoughtful. And since I'm always being pegged as a bit of a geek for getting high marks and knowing stuff, I look for guys who have more than half a functioning brain cell. It's nice when you can talk about things other than whether a certain team is going to win the NBA season, or if Rihanna should've went back to Chris Brown.

Suddenly, he locks eyes with me.

"Hello, darlin'!" he shouts. "Like what you see, then?" Then he pokes his tongue out at me and begins rapidly flicking it up and down. "Why don't you come over here and give us a kiss?"

The rest of the boys around him burst out laughing.

My cheeks are burning embers. So much for my hypothesis about this guy being intelligent. My embarrassment rapidly turns into anger. I envision walking over and punching him in the face or grabbing a handful of that dishevelled blond hair and pulling it as hard as I can. I imagine the look of surprise on his face, the shame and embarrassment he'd feel in front of his friends. And, though there's no guarantee, most guys still don't hit girls, so I figure it would be a win-win situation for me.

"Don't mind them," a soft voice from behind me says.

I whirl around. Standing only a few centimetres away from me is this freaky-looking girl. She's watching me so intently it gives me the creeps. Part of the creepy feeling comes from her appearance. She's incredibly thin and as pale as a dead fish. Her bony arms jut out, twig-like, from the sleeves of a black T-shirt that is so faded, it's nearly grey. To top it off, I notice the round scabs running up and down the inside skin of her forearms. Gross.

"I'm Imogen," she says, sticking out one of her

scrawny hands in my direction. With her other hand, she pushes the thick glasses she's wearing farther up the bridge of her long nose. I notice that black electrical tape is the only thing holding the right arm of her glasses onto the frames.

What a freak. She actually wants me to shake her hand? Weirdness seems to be this girl Imogen's thing, so I go along with it, already wondering how to get away from her.

"I'm Edie."

The palm of her hand feels moist. I have to stop myself from gagging. Instinctively I wipe my hand up and down the front of my navy skirt as soon she lets go.

Imogen runs a hand through her thin, blond hair, cocks her head to one side and continues to study me. Her hair is so thin it's almost translucent. Creepy doesn't even begin to cover this girl.

"That's an unusual name. Kind of Andy Warhol. Are you from Hollywood?"

"No," I reply.

"What year are you in?"

"Year?" I ask. Then I remember. They don't go by grades here. "Year Ten."

"Me, too!" Imogen squeals. If she gets this excited because I'm in the same grade as her, I wonder what she'd be like if she won the lottery. Clearly friends are in short supply for this girl.

The bell sounds. I've never been so glad to have a school day begin.

"See you around," I say, turning and walking toward the front entrance of the school.

Instead of getting the hint, she scurries up beside me like a cockroach.

"Where are you from then?"

"Toronto," I answer. She's really beginning to get on my nerves. I don't like it when people ask too many questions. The less people know, the safer it is for both Mom and I.

"Where's that?"

"It's in Ontario."

"Is that in America?"

I grit my teeth. "No … it's a province in Canada."

"Oh," she replies with a dismissive shrug of her bony shoulders. "'Cos you sound as though you're from Hollywood. After you," she offers, struggling to hold one of the heavy front doors open for me while balancing her binder and books. I wonder why she hasn't invested in a knapsack like sane people.

As I step through the doorway, I'm shoved aside by a group of girls pushing through. One of them turns sideways as she moves past Imogen, nearly knocking her over.

The girl glances back at us.

"You best watch where you're going, Maggots," she says a smirk playing across her face.

Imogen reddens, readjusts the books in her arms, and then stares down at her feet.

The girl tosses her dark red-and-black braids behind one shoulder and fastens her eyes on me. I glare back at her.

"Why look!" she squeals with mock delight. "Maggots got herself a friend this year!" The group of girls begins laughing in unison. What a bunch of lemmings.

"Shut up," I snap, narrowing my eyes. I look her up and down with a glare of disgust. "You don't even know me."

She places her hands on her hips and glares back at me. Her upper lip curls away from her teeth, giving her this rabid-dog look.

"I don't know you, huh? Well, you obviously don't know who *I am*." She sucks her teeth loudly to emphasize her point. "You're just lucky I need to get to class, tough girl. Else we'd have ourselves a little introducing right here and now."

With that she strides away, followed closely by her friends.

Imogen and I wait a few seconds before walking into the school. I think both of us want to avoid any further confrontation with the girls though I'm so angry I could punch walls. I'm feeling all shaky from the adrenaline and force myself to take some deep breaths to calm down.

I try to get my mind off of what just happened by taking in my new surroundings. The school is old and huge. With all the English accents and uniforms, it's kind of like being on the set of a Harry Potter movie. Hundreds of students move through the cavernous foyer, their voices echoing loudly off the walls. Sharp pangs of homesickness wash over me.

"I can't believe you did that," Imogen says. She's watching me with a look somewhere between awe and fear plastered across her face.

"She deserved it," I say with a shrug of my shoulders. "What I can't believe is the way you let her push you around. It's pathetic."

Imogen stops walking and hugs her binder against her chest. Her bottom lip quivers. For a moment, I feel ashamed. The putdown was completely uncalled for.

"What choice do I have? Most of us just try to stay clear of Precious and hope she doesn't notice us."

"Her name is *Precious*?"

"Yeah. Precious. Precious Samuel."

"And you're really that afraid of her?"

Sensing that my nastiness is done, Imogen nods enthusiastically, causing her broken glasses to slide down the bridge of her nose again. She's like a puppy dog — so eager to please.

"Why?" I ask. There's no way I'd ever let anyone treat me like that.

"Precious and her lot are cows. You need to watch out for them. Last year Precious broke this girl's jaw at the Riverdale Centre. It's the big shopping mall by the roundabout."

Imogen doesn't realize that all these landmarks mean nothing to me. The longing to be back in Regent, back where I belong, hits me again.

"Broke her jaw?" I ask. "She's so skinny she looks like she'd snap in two in a strong wind. Anyway, nobody scares me." Nobody but *him*, I think.

Imogen looks around as though checking to make sure no one is overhearing our conversation.

"She goes crazy sometimes, Edie. Absolutely nutters."

Another bell rings, sending several students scurrying up the nearby stairwell.

"Pants! It's the second bell already," Imogen moans. "What form are you in?"

"I don't know. They told my mom I had to go the office first to find out because I was a late register."

"Oh, okay," Imogen replies. "I'm in A204 with Mr. Smith. Fingers crossed that we're together!" She turns to go, waving enthusiastically over her shoulder at me.

I smile half-heartedly back at her. Walking toward the doors to the main office, I cross my fingers, hoping to be placed in any homeroom class other than A204. I definitely don't want that girl thinking she's my new best friend.

# CHAPTER 4

I spot her straight away. Dark braids, dark eyes. Glaring at me as I stand in the doorway like a fool. Great. Precious is in my homeroom class.

"Ms. Bryans?" Mr. Middleton, the headteacher, says.

I feel sick. Why doesn't he just let me walk into the class? I don't want an introduction. Especially not when the entire room is staring at me like I'm some kind of a drooling science experiment.

Ms. Bryans turns around. A cluster of thick, black curls sit tightly on top of her head like a wig that's two sizes too small. Dark slashes pulled low on her forehead serve as eyebrows and the shadow of a moustache dances above her upper lip.

"Class, say good morning to Mr. Middleton," she says.

"Good morning, Mr. Middleton," a few students mumble unenthusiastically.

He smiles. "Good morning everyone. We have a new student from Canada joining us today."

The class continues to stare blankly at me. So much for just blending in. I look down at a black smear of chewing gum on the floor near the toe of my shoe. Warmth radiates from my face.

"This is Edith."

"Edie," I whisper. "Just Edie. It's not short for anything."

"Sorry … um. Edie. This is Edie."

Muffled laughter from the back of the class; Precious is sitting back there.

"She's moved here all the way from Ontario. That means I'm expecting all of you," he pauses, gazing sternly at the students seated in the back rows of the room, "to make her feel welcome."

Ms. Bryans gives me an impatient half-smile. Clearly she isn't pleased to have an addition to the class.

"Welcome, Edie. Please take a seat. We're just reviewing school policies." She looks at Mr. Middleton. "Academic?" she says, raising an eyebrow.

"Her mother only provided us with one report," he answers. "We're waiting on the rest of her academic files to be sent. But from what we have, yes."

I look around for an empty seat as far away from Precious Samuel as possible. A girl sitting close to the front of the classroom waves at me.

"You can sit beside me," she offers.

"Thank you, Savitri," Ms. Bryans says, walking over to her desk and picking up a pile of papers. She hands them to an acne-riddled boy in the front row.

"Please take a term schedule and then pass them along."

I dash to the empty seat, grateful to no longer be the centre of attention.

"Hi," Savitri whispers as I sit down. Her teeth are Chiclet white, her eyes heavy with black eyeliner.

"Thanks so much for saving me."

"Not a worry," she says with a wink. Her eyelashes are so long they almost touch her eyebrows. "I would've died if Middleton did that to me."

The rest of the morning passes uneventfully. As lunch break gets closer, a familiar nervous feeling begins to develop in the pit of my stomach. Lunch in a new school is always awkward. All the cliques and groups are already established and a packed cafeteria is the last place anyone wants to be seen alone.

A few minutes before the bell sounds, Savitri turns to me.

"Are you eating lunch here?" she asks.

"I guess so. I brought money, but don't really know any places around here to grab lunch. You?"

"I'm meeting my friends in the cafeteria. Come eat with us."

I breathe a sigh of relief and begin to gather my books together. Maybe things aren't going to be that bad; maybe Mom is right — I just need to be more optimistic. More a glass-half-full kind of girl.

The bell sounds. The room immediately fills with the clatter of chairs being shoved away from desks.

"Thanks, that would be great," I say, gathering my books together.

"My friends are brilliant, but I know they'll have a million questions to ask you about Canada. Just tell them to shut it if they get on your nerves."

The cafeteria is heaving with bodies. Students rush back and forth between tables, waving and yelling at friends as they enter the room.

"Keisha, this is Edie," Savitri says as we sit down with our trays at a table near the middle of the room. "She's from Canada."

Keisha looks up from the mountain of French fries she's devouring and gives me a wide smile. "Oh yeah? I've got cousins in Canada. In Toronto, I think."

That sudden twist of homesickness in my stomach is back.

"Really? I'm from Toronto," I say with forced brightness.

Keisha stabs several ketchup-coated fries with her fork. "I've never been to see my cousins though. I only met them once at a wedding in Jamaica. I'd love to go to Toronto someday."

"Hi, Edie," a familiar voice interrupts. "How's everything so far?'

I look up. Imogen is hovering nervously beside our table. She's holding her plastic lunch tray so tightly her knuckles have turned bone white. Her plate is heaped with fries and some sort of breaded, egg-shaped thing that smells like a combination of dirty gym socks and pickles. I wrinkle my nose at the stench.

I don't want to be mean, but I also don't want

any more trouble from Precious and her cronies and Imogen seems to attract bullies like rotten food attracts flies.

"Um, it was okay," I answer. Both Keisha and Savitri are completely ignoring Imogen. Savitri is staring so hard at her salad you'd think a secret message was hidden amongst the wilted lettuce and bits of unripe tomato.

"Oh. That's good to hear," Imogen replies, nodding her head at me. "Hi, Savitri. Hi, Keisha. All right?"

Savitri glances up from her salad. "Fine," she says, her voice curt.

Imogen shifts her weight from foot to foot. It's obvious to me that she knows she's not wanted, but has no idea how to get out of here gracefully. I feel badly because she's never done anything to me. In fact, she's gone out of her way to talk to me and make me feel welcome at the school. If I were a better person, I'd invite her to sit down and have lunch with us.

But I'm not.

"Okay. So I guess we'll see you later," I say.

Imogen's face crumples. For a moment I'm afraid she might cry.

"Um, sure. Okay." Her tray shakes ever so slightly. "Have a nice lunch, then." She turns and disappears into the chaos of the cafeteria.

"Bloody time she left!" Keisha says. "What a loser Maggots is! I can't believe she's in my homeroom this year."

"Well, we've got Precious Samuels and Jermaine Lewis in ours, so count yourself lucky," Savitri replies. "At least your class isn't full of psychos."

Keisha laughs through a forkful of fries. "That is pretty awful."

"Who's Jermaine Lewis?" I ask.

"He wasn't here this morning," Savitri says. "Misses loads of school. Doesn't really matter though 'cos he's always in trouble when he is here. I don't even know why he's in academic with all of us. He's as thick as a brick wall."

"And when he was eight," Keisha whispers, lowering her head so that her chin nearly knocks against the table as she speaks, "He killed a bunch of kids, including his own brother."

Jermaine Lewis arrives after lunch. It seems he's in my math class as well as homeroom. He strolls in fifteen minutes into the lesson without a word, his gaze traveling slowly around the room, searching for an empty place. No one raises a hand to offer him a seat.

I try not to stare but can't help myself. Some kids I knew back in Regent Park were involved in gangs and dealing; things that sometimes led to their own deaths or jail, but not many were involved in anything as serious as murder.

Jermaine glances at me. Mild curiosity flashes across his face. I look away as he sits down near Savitri and me. Although he doesn't seem to care about being late for class, our math teacher, Mr. O'Connor, clearly does.

"How kind of you to join us, Mr. Lewis," he says, stopping the lesson in mid-sentence. "Forget to set your alarm clock?"

Jermaine doesn't answer; he just sits, silently gazing back.

The class is suddenly focused in a way we haven't been for any of part of the algebra lesson. We're all waiting for Mr. O'Connor's next move.

"I asked you a question, Jermaine."

Nothing.

Splotchy crimson patches appear on the teacher's chest and neck. His chin wiggles a bit.

"I'm waiting," he says, folding his arms across his chest. This only serves to emphasize his man breasts and the wet pit stains on his shirt.

Silence. Someone at the front of the room coughs loudly to disguise a giggle.

"I'm waiting for you to drop this useless attitude and tell me why you're so late for class. And on the first day of school." Spittle flies from his lips. "Not the best way to start Year Ten, is it?"

There should be a handbook for all teachers. One that tells them very clearly to never, ever confront a student in front of other students.

"I had to do something for my mum," Jermaine suddenly replies. His voice is level, but there is an edge to his words, a warning to Mr. O'Connor to back off.

"Well, clearly I need to ring your mother and remind her of the importance of getting an education." Mr. O'Connor says, rolling his eyes before turning back to the white board to continue scribbling down algebraic equations.

Savitri leans over. "He's such a rude twat."

I nod in agreement. It's difficult to concentrate on the math lesson after that. I have trouble with math at the best of times as it never really makes sense to me, but now my attention keeps wandering back to Jermaine. He keeps his head down, focusing on whatever is in his desk, rather than on Mr. O'Connor. How could you blame him? I still don't understand why he'd made Jermaine's lateness into such a big deal. Lots of other students were being disruptive during class, but they were hardly spoken to.

At the end of the day, Savitri and I meet up with Keisha in the girls' toilets on the first floor.

"What are you two doing now?" Savitri asks from inside one of the stalls.

"I've got to go home," I reply. Mom will be super worried if I'm late.

Keisha shakes her head. "Not me. I'm going to the leisure centre until they kick me out. That way my mum can't stick me looking after my little brothers and sisters for once." She kisses her teeth, fumbles around in her purse, and takes out a silver tube of lipstick.

"You got any brothers or sisters, Edie?" she asks, coating her full lips bright crimson.

"No. It's just my mom and me."

I check out my reflection in the mirror. I left most of my makeup behind in Toronto. Mom and

I are sharing hers until we have money to replace it. My eyeliner is faded and I look tired. So much for good first impressions.

"Lucky you," Savitri says as she emerges from the bathroom stall.

I gasp. Savitri's long, ebony hair is hidden under a black hijab and her face is devoid of any trace of makeup.

"I know, I know," she says, rolling her eyes. "My brother Amir and Dad would kill me if they knew what I look like at school."

As I walk home after saying goodbye to Savitri and Keisha, I remind myself not to become too attached. After all, things are sure to change. And I need to keep a low profile so that Mom and I will be as safe as possible. I cross my fingers. Please let this be the last move.

# CHAPTER 5

"So, how was it?" Mom asks, her voice floating out from the tiny living room at the front of the flat.

I slide my knapsack from my shoulders. It hits the floor with a thud. Though the front hall is carpeted, it's so thin and worn the wooden planks underneath show through in patches.

"It was okay, I guess." I walk to the doorway of the living room and lean against the doorjamb.

My mother's sitting on the edge of the sofa, an assortment of papers strewn all around her.

"Just okay?" She looks up at me and pats a spot on the sofa beside her. "Come and tell me all about it."

The flat came fully furnished, but the furniture is ancient and worn. I wonder if the owner is waiting for it to disintegrate before buying anything new. And everything made out of fabric smells musty, like beach towels that haven't dried properly.

Mom shuffles some of the papers into makeshift piles, clearing off a larger space for me to sit.

"So, how was it, really?"

I notice the dark smudges under her eyes and the way the skin at the outer corners crinkles like autumn leaves when she smiles at me. She looks older with every passing day.

"It was good."

I don't want to add to her worries. I sit and tug at the navy tie that is part of our school uniform, trying to loosen its grip on my neck.

Mom cocks her head sideways and looks at me hard. "Be honest, Edie."

"It's just kind of different, you know? Like, why do I have to wear this tie? The entire day I felt like I was being hung."

"I think the word is hanged," Mom says with a laugh. She reaches over, playfully ruffling my hair. I gently swat her hand away.

"Hey! Are you too old to be hugged?" she asks.

I shrug. "No. I'm just so tired of being the new kid. And I wish I understood how stuff works here."

"These things take time, sweetheart. You always make friends wherever we go."

"Yeah, just in time to leave again."

Hurt briefly flashes in my mother's eyes.

"I didn't really mean it," I mumble, staring down at my hands. God, why do I always have to be so hurtful? "What are you doing?" I ask, hoping to change the conversation.

Mom pauses for a moment before answering.

"Just sorting though some bills to be sure I paid

everything off in Toronto. In case we ever have to go back."

I nod. We can't have our mail forwarded from Canada. It's too dangerous to put a change of address file in with the post office; that would make it too easy to trace our steps here.

"I know this is a big challenge, Edie. But I still think it was the right decision to move here. Once we've been here without any incidents for a year, I'll put things into motion and get a real job with a decent salary."

"We've hardly lasted a year anywhere."

Her eyes darken. She presses her lips together so that they look like two bloodless worms.

"Then we'll be able to rent a flat on our own," she continues, though her voice is now strained. "And move out of here. I have a really good feeling this time."

I try to smile, but my face feels frozen, like the last time I went to see the dentist and he stuck a needle into my gums. I want to believe Mom, but there have just been too many times when things seemed good, even better than good. And then everything would all fall apart again. He'd find us. We'd run.

"I should start my homework," I say. I really don't want to discuss the future. After all, the future doesn't include my friends in Toronto or Peaches or anything that really matters to me.

"We're survivors," she says, placing her arm around my shoulder and giving me a squeeze.

This time I don't resist. I can't stand to see that look of hurt in her eyes again.

"In fact, I'll have you know that your old mom has already landed herself a job. What do you think of that?"

I glance up. "It's good … I suppose. What's the job?"

"Well," Mom begins, settling back against the couch. She pulls me back with her. "Sit and relax for a minute, silly!"

A spring from the couch pokes at my back like an anorexic finger.

"I'm going to be cleaning swank office buildings in the heart of London."

I listen as my mother tries to make the new job sound decent. But I'm not buying it. She has two university degrees. Cleaning offices is a far cry from what she's qualified to do.

"There's only one little drawback to the job. Since I need to get paid under the table, I have to work the night shift for the first while."

I open my mouth to protest, but shut it again.

"It means you'll be on your own a bit more. Are you okay with that?"

Like I have a choice.

"I guess you have to find some way to get us food and stuff," I mumble.

"Remember, it's only going to be for a short while. And speaking of food," she says, standing up and putting her hands on her hips. "I bought us a lovely roast chicken for dinner to celebrate."

My stomach does a hungry somersault. I haven't eaten since lunch.

"I think that homework can wait, don't you?" Mom asks, giving me a hug.

I want so badly to believe that she's right; that everything is going to be okay. But I just can't.

# CHAPTER 6

I wrinkle my nose. The smell of damp fills my nostrils. I roll over and bury my face deep into my pillow.

My bedroom door opens.

"Wake up, sleepyhead!" Mom calls from the doorway.

I force my head up from the pillow.

"We'll get you some blinds with my first pay." Mom says. She walks in and sits on the edge of the bed. "I'll be gone to work before you get in from school this afternoon, but I'll leave food in the fridge for dinner. Just be sure to turn the cooker off when you're done using it."

*Cooker? It's a stove!* I want to scream. Instead, I swing out of bed and stumble to the bathroom. The cold tiles of the floor jolt any remaining drowsiness out of me.

The small bathroom makes me feel claustrophobic. I turn on the tap, splash water on my face, and undress.

A faint knocking sound comes from the other side of the door. I consider turning on the shower and not answering it, but Mom knocks again, this time a little more loudly. I wrap a towel around myself, open the door a crack, and stick my head out.

My mother smiles at me. "I just want to let you know that I love you more than anything in this world."

"You needed to pull me out of the shower and make me late for school just to tell me that?"

"I felt it was important that you know." She leans in and kisses me on the cheek. "Now get into that shower and get to school so you can someday rule the world, Edie Fraser!"

The walk to school is interesting and uncomfortable all at once; so many things are unfamiliar and I almost feel like a baby again, having to learn about this new country. Will I ever get used to the accents, to the way cars drive on the wrong side of the street, or the fact that there isn't a Tim Hortons anywhere in sight?

It's another wet day and the sidewalks are slick with rain. I hate the way the clouds hang so low in the sky here. There's so little light, the street lamps have stayed on.

"Watch out, you stupid cow!"

Pain blooms across my left shoulder.

Another shove sends me stumbling backward against a black, wrought-iron fence. My knapsack drops to the ground. At least five girls surround me. I don't recognize any of them, except one.

"Fancy yourself better than us, do ya?" Precious sneers. She takes a step toward me.

"No." I say, trying to keep my voice steady.

"Yeah? Well, we caught you giving us cut-eye yesterday," one of the other girls says. She narrows her eyes at me. "Either that or you're staring at us 'cos you're completely gay."

"That's it, innit?" Precious says, leaning so close to me that I can feel the warmth of her breath against my face. It smells faintly of eggs, which makes me want to gag. "Do you want a kiss?"

One of them picks up my knapsack. "Let's see if the poxy little American did her homework last night. Bets that she did!"

Squeals of delight emanate from the pack of girls as they turn my bag upside down. Its contents spill out onto the sidewalk.

Through a haze of tears I notice adults scurrying along, stepping around us. They hold their umbrellas high as they rush toward the nearby train station. Do adults forget what it was like to be a teenager, to be bullied?

I hold my breath, trying to prevent myself from sobbing. If I cry, it will only make things worse.

"What's this rubbish?" the girl who dumped my knapsack asks. She's holding my journal. My heart twists inside my chest. My journal contains all my letters to Rume. All my secrets.

"Isn't this sweet?" Precious says, grabbing my journal out of the girl's hand.

She opens it up to a random page.

"Dear Rume," she begins, placing a hand on her hip and reading each word with an exaggerated Texan drawl. "I know you'll wonder where I've gone and why I left without even saying goodbye ..."

"Stop it!" I yell, my voice catching in my throat. Everything is blurring, tears threatening to leap from my lower lids. If she reads just a little farther in my diary, they'll find out everything.

I lunge toward Precious. For a moment she looks completely surprised. Then two of the girls grab me by the arms and thrust me back against the fence.

"Shut it!" one of them hisses, giving me a quick jab in the chest with her index finger.

"Awww," Precious says. "What's the matter, Texas? You don't want me to read your love letters to your girlfriend? Do you write about getting off with her in here?"

Fury claws at my chest. "Bitch!" I scream.

"Look here! Oi! You lot! Leave that girl alone, do you hear?"

A burly man in paint-splattered coveralls heads toward us from across the street. He looks like a grizzly bear wrapped in a Jackson Pollock painting. Relief floods through my body as he approaches.

"You're bloody lucky," Precious says, throwing my journal down on the ground. She turns and runs. The other girls follow. The one that poked me in the chest takes a second to grind my homework under the toes of her shoes before leaving.

I bend down and carefully retrieve my diary. Then I try to salvage what I can of my homework assignment. Most of it is soggy and dirty, the ink smeared into unreadable black blotches.

"You okay?" the man asks. He bends down to help me. I can smell his cologne. It reminds me of the cheap aftershave the boys in Regent Park used to spray up and down the school hallways in the hope of causing at least one teacher to have an allergic reaction.

I nod at him. Tears spill down my cheeks. With one hand I brush them away.

"Thanks," I stammer as we stand up.

"No need," he replies. "You American? Is that why they're taking the piss?"

I have no idea what he means. "I'm Canadian," I reply as I stuff my schoolwork, or what's left of it, back into my knapsack. "Thanks again for everything. I better get to school. I think I'm officially late."

The man cocks his head sideways and gives me a long look. "You're shaking. Are you certain you're all right?"

I nod back. "Yeah. I'm sure."

I begin walking up the hill toward school, uncertain what Precious and her friends might have in store for me when I arrive, but vow to keep my anger in check.

# CHAPTER 7

I clutch the late slip to my chest, open the classroom door, and step inside, taking care to be as quiet as possible.

Ms. Bryans stops her lesson mid-sentence, a stumpy piece of chalk hanging between her thumb and forefinger like a cigarette.

"You're late, Miss Fraser," she says.

Tell me something I don't know. I can feel her eyes judging me, taking in the wet, matted mess of my hair, the soggy notebook, and dishevelled school uniform.

"Where is your late slip?"

"Right here." I hold out the piece of yellow paper. It's soaked from being held against my sweater.

Ms. Bryans breathes audibly out her nose. "Place it in the recycling bin, Edie. Then quickly take your seat. I think you've wasted more than enough of our class time today."

"Sorry," I reply.

"Apology accepted. Of course you'll join me at lunch for detention."

I nod, hoping Ms. Bryans's head will spontaneously combust as I walk to my seat.

The morning's lessons drag on at an excruciating pace. I hold my breath each time I change classes, anticipating Precious and her posse around every corner. But she doesn't show to homeroom English, and, as the morning wears on, it becomes evident that she is likely skipping classes for the day. Maybe she thinks I'm going to report what happened to the headmaster or another adult at the school. But I'm not stupid. There's no way I want to become known as a rat.

It's only when the lunch bell rings that I remember my detention. I slam my books down on the desk and kick my chair back.

"What's wrong with you?" Savitri asks.

"Just this stupid detention I have with Ms. Bryans. I guess I'll catch up with you and Keisha after school." The injustice of the situation makes me angry; I'm paying the price for Precious's bullying when I haven't done anything.

"Ms. Bryans has got to let you at least buy your lunch," Savitri says. "Come on, I'll walk down to the lunchroom with you."

The door to the classroom is slightly ajar when I come back from the cafeteria. Balancing my tray carefully, I nudge the door open with the toe of my shoe.

Ms. Bryans is at her desk, hunched over a stack

of papers. From the doorway, she looks tinier than usual. I notice her green cardigan hangs awkwardly on her tiny shoulders like it's been washed one too many times.

For a moment, I swear she looks sad. That changes as soon as she notices me; her eyes narrow and she regards me with a look usually reserved for dog shit smeared on the bottom of shoes.

"Thank you for politely knocking, Edie. I'd expect nothing less from you."

"Sorry." I reach over and knock on the door, feeling completely stupid. What did I do to make her hate me so much?

Ms. Bryans waves me in. "Never mind now. Sit down. At least you're on time, unlike Mr. Lewis. Find something useful to do." She picks up her pen and begins marking the pile of papers again.

I sit down and slowly unzip my knapsack. The way Ms. Bryans spat out Jermaine's name, it seems like just saying it makes her want to vomit. Why does she continue to teach? It's pretty obvious she doesn't like kids much.

My journal is still in my bag. I reach down and grab it. It's the only way I can feel like I have any kind of contact with Rume right now. I wonder when Mom will feel it's safe to send an email to Rume so I can tell her why I disappeared.

"Jermaine! So nice to see you."

In my peripheral vision, I see him standing in the doorway. I don't look up.

"Sorry I'm late."

Ms. Bryans laughs. "So am I, so am I, Jermaine. I was looking forward to spending much more time with you."

Jermaine takes a few hesitant steps forward. "I had to go home. My mother needed her medicine from the chemist."

"You mother again? I'm sure she needed her *medicine* from the off-licence, I mean chemist. Now can you please take your seat and make yourself useful?"

As he walks into the room, I raise my head and quickly glance at him. He catches my eye and smiles. Heat blooms across my cheeks. I look back at the page in front of me and read the words I've scrawled there.

*Dear Rume, I hate this place so much and totally miss you and Toronto and the sunshine there.*

"Of course, you'll need to serve the time you missed for today's detention at tomorrow's lunch," Ms. Bryans adds.

Jermaine shrugs, plunks himself down onto the seat directly in front of me, and reaches into his bag. He pulls out a notebook and book. Pretending to contemplate my next sentence, I chew on the end of my pen and casually lean sideways, trying to get a better view of him. He opens the notebook and starts to write.

I lean farther to the left, craning my neck to see what novel he's reading.

"Miss Fraser, what exactly are you doing?" Ms. Bryans asks.

"Nothing," I reply, sitting back in my seat.

"Really?" She smiles like a barracuda. "It looked to me like you were very interested in what Mr. Lewis was doing a moment ago."

*Bitch.*

"Jermaine, what's on your desk that is so interesting?"

He stops writing. This is horrible.

"I just wanted to see what he's reading," I say.

Jermaine turns around in his seat. "Tupac's *The Rose That Grew from the Concrete*. It's a book of his poetry." He hands it to me. "Have a look."

I take the book. "Thanks."

It makes no sense. Ms. Bryans and other teachers at this school treat Jermaine like he's completely retarded, as though he couldn't read a fourth-grade chapter book to save his life. I'm beginning to learn that students aren't the only bullies at Windrush School.

A few minutes before the end of the lunch period, Ms. Bryans stands up. She walks over to us and sits on top of the desk directly in front of Jermaine, crossing her legs primly at the ankles. In her hands she's holding the coffee can our class is using to collect donations for an outreach project that is building a girls' school in Pakistan. Dark hairs peek out like spider's legs from beneath the sleeves of her cardigan.

"The two of you can go and get ready for your afternoon classes," she says dryly. "And Ms. Fraser?"

"Yes?"

"I really think you should endeavour to make a better impression around here. We have no records from your former school in Toronto yet, but you strike me as a clever girl. In other words, don't let yourself be influenced by some of the students here who exhibit … less than desirable behaviours." She raises an eyebrow in Jermaine's direction as she speaks.

Then, with a dismissive wave of her hand, we're excused from the class.

"A moment please, Edie."

I stop in the doorway. Jermaine is already half-way down the hall, his long legs carrying him away from Ms. Bryans as quickly as possible.

I wince and turn around. What now?

Ms. Bryans stands regarding me sternly, her arms folded across her chest.

"Why don't we have the OSR from your old school yet? School records can be sent electronically, you know."

"Oh?" I say, feigning surprise. "I had no idea."

"Is there anything you'd like to tell me, Edie?"

A cold lightning bolt of fear shoots through my body.

"No. Why would there be?" I try to keep my voice as steady as possible.

She tilts her head and regards me carefully. I wonder if she's one of those people who can detect when someone isn't being completely honest. Is my eye twitching involuntarily or something?

"I was just wondering if I should make a phone

call to your old school to see if they had concerns with your punctuality or anything else ..."

"You don't need to do that," I interject. Though my mind is speeding like a Japanese bullet train toward panic mode, I try to keep my voice slow and steady. "My old school is really busy and I was the least of their worries. Believe me."

Ms. Bryans smiles triumphantly. "Then I guess I'll see you tomorrow at 8:40 sharp, Ms. Fraser."

# CHAPTER 8

The stench of urine burns my nostrils as I trudge up the stairwell to the third-floor landing of our building. Everything is grey concrete, bleak and indistinguishable, aside from the different colours of the front doors. Mom and I live in flat 14. It has a red door. Depressing doesn't even begin to describe this place.

I'm freezing. The light drizzle has dampened my hair, making strands of it stick to my cheeks like overcooked spaghetti. Already I am sick of rain and the thick curtain of cloud that is perpetually drawn across London's sky. I reach under my sweater and pull out the key to the flat.

It's Mom's first night at her new job. I wish she were waiting inside the apartment for me with cups of hot chocolate for us to share. Though I wouldn't worry her by telling her what happened in the morning with Precious and her gang and then with Ms. Bryans, just her presence would make me feel better.

Once inside, I strip off my sweater and hang it

over the radiator. The radiator, once white, is now badly chipped and mottled with rust. Then I turn on all the first-floor lights. Somehow the brightness makes me feel a little less lonely.

Darkness comes so much earlier here than in Canada. This has something to do with latitude and longitude. Mom says London is farther north than Toronto, even though winters are colder in Canada. She's promised she'll take me to Greenwich Park and the observatory so I can stand on the Prime Meridian line and be in two time zones at once. I wish I could tell Rume I'm going to do that. She loves Indian astrology and anything astronomy-related.

After a dinner of leftover chicken, I finish my homework in the living room then curl up on the sofa and watch television. There's not really anything on, but I don't want to go upstairs yet. Pulling a blanket around me, I rest my head against a cushion and try not to think about the fact that I'm going to have to spend more nights like this, all alone. Besides, we're finally safe. There's no way he'll find us here.

I wake up as the room brightens. The thin curtains allow the morning light to stream into the room. It's been so long since I've seen sunshine, that I immediately feel happy. I stretch my arms above my head and sit up. My shoulder and neck ache from sleeping on the lumpy couch. Tonight, I'll have to force myself to sleep in my own bed. Yawning, I make my way to the kitchen for some juice. As I open the fridge door, the digital clock on the microwave catches my eye.

Eight o'clock!

Adrenaline shoots through my body, leaving me cold and shaky. Forty minutes until classes start. I can't be late or else Ms. Bryans will start snooping into my business for sure.

I gulp down a glass of orange juice and run upstairs, taking the steps two at a time. After a quick glance at my reflection in the mirrored door of my wardrobe, I decide to skip taking a shower and just throw my hair back into a ponytail.

If I'm late again, Ms. Bryans will lose it for sure. The last thing I want is for her to call here and bug Mom to come in and discuss things. Mom doesn't need more worries. And she certainly doesn't need to be woken up after working all night. I look at my watch. Eight-fifteen.

Mom said she'd get off at six every morning and be home in plenty of time to see me before school.

So where is she?

# CHAPTER 9

I make it to class just as the morning bell sounds. My tongue is thick in my mouth from running the entire way along the high street and up the hill to school but there isn't a second to spare for a drink.

As I walk through the doorway to class, I feel a sudden, painful jab between my shoulder blades. I whirl around.

"Sorry about that, Texas."

Precious. She's holding a binder in her hands with one of its corners jutting towards me. She smiles. It's a smile that doesn't reach her eyes and seems full of violent promises.

Before I can even react, an unfamiliar voice interrupts us. Considering the fact that I was about two seconds away from punching Precious in the face, I guess it's a good thing.

"Ladies! Inside immediately and take a seat before I mark you late!"

Gritting my teeth, I walk away from Precious

and into the room. In order to save face, I'm going to have to stand up to Precious sooner rather than later. The problem is, though I want nothing more than to feel the skin of her jawbone connecting with my fist, I need to stay out of trouble. Why doesn't she just leave me alone?

I sit down at my desk. The class is practically humming with anticipation. Substitute teachers guarantee a day full of the worst behaviour a class can conjure up. Personally, I'm just relieved to have a break from Ms. Bryans.

"Hey, girl," Savitri says. "This one's new. She doesn't stand a chance. Even really experienced teachers have walked out of our school."

The teacher walks up to the front of the room, picks up a piece of chalk and writes her name across the blackboard in large, block letters.

MS. THELWELL

"All right, everyone!" she says, turning back around. "Settle yourselves and quiet down to listen to morning announcements."

"Did you know you're hot, Miss?" someone near the back shouts out. I turn around. It's the boy who nearly decapitated me with a soccer ball the first day of school. Everyone laughs.

"Leave it to Rodney to play the fool," Savitri says, rolling her eyes.

Ms. Thelwell doesn't even flinch. Maybe Savitri's wrong about her.

"Fifteen-minute detention for you after class today," she says.

Rodney sits back down. He looks both angry and confused all at once.

Ms. Thelwell asks two students to hand out our novel study questions. We're reading a book called *Journey to Jo'burg*. I love the book even though it's way below my reading level. It's set during Apartheid in South Africa and revolves around a girl named Naledi who has to go and find her mother in Johannesburg because her baby brother is dying. I'd read a bit of it last night before falling asleep on the sofa. Today I want nothing to do with a book about a girl being separated from her mother.

A white blur flies by my face. It passes so close, I can feel the air in its wake whisper against my cheek. Several moments later the paper projectile collides with its intended target: Ms. Thelwell's head.

For a moment it sits wedged in the teacher's fiery curls. She slowly reaches up to retrieve it. There's writing scribbled down one side of the paper. Ms. Thelwell reads it and reddens before violently crumpling the paper in her hand.

"This," she says, "is tantamount to sexual harassment and I need to know who wrote it immediately." She scans the room, meeting the gaze of as many students as possible. No one says a word.

"That's fine," she says, her voice trembling slightly. "It's fine because until the person responsible for this comes forward and demonstrates to me that he or she is not a complete coward, the entire lot of you will serve a thirty-minute detention after classes today."

There's a massive groan from the class, but Ms. Thelwell still doesn't get the answer she's looking for. No one is willing to be a rat. The bell sounds for second period.

"Go to your next class," she says. "But I still expect the person who did this to see me before the end of the day. Or else I will be seeing all of you."

"That Irish cow isn't going to tell me what I can and can't do with my time after school," Precious snarls to no one in particular as we file out the door. Her face is a mask of fury. "My mum is expecting me home. So, I'd like to see that woman just try to make me stay."

Her comment makes me think of Mom again. She should've been home before I left for school. I know traffic in London can be really bad and that Mom was taking buses to save money rather than the subway or trains but still … the night shift was supposed to end at 6 a.m. Two hours was more than enough time to get back to our apartment.

"You're really quiet today," Savitri says, interrupting my thoughts.

"I'm just tired." I want to tell her about Mom not being home, but know I shouldn't.

"Are you sure that's it?" she asks. I wonder what she thinks is bothering me. She wouldn't believe the truth if I told her.

"Yeah, I hear you. I just really want this day to be over so I can get home to sleep. Rodney better tell that teacher that he threw the stupid airplane or I'll slap him into next week."

When Ms. Thelwell finally dismisses us, I say goodbye to Savitri and then run out of the school. Both Precious and her friend Shandel didn't even show up for detention. If Ms. Thelwell noticed they weren't there, she certainly didn't show it. I wish I'd just left when the bell rang too.

As soon as I get home, I drop my knapsack in the hallway and rush into the kitchen. Nothing's been touched. My juice glass from the morning is still sitting on the counter exactly where I'd left it, the ghostly remains of a watermark visible around its base. My hairbrush is perched on the edge of the sink. One thing about Mom is that she's a neat freak. She would've washed the glass, put the hairbrush back into the wicker basket upstairs in the bathroom, and then nagged me endlessly about the fact that hairbrushes had no place in kitchens. She'd have told me to tidy as best I could before leaving for school in the morning …

But she hasn't been back.

I rush out of the kitchen into the living room. No sign of Mom having been there, either. Cold fingers of fear close around my heart. It's impossible. Maybe she just came home and slept. She'd be exhausted after working the night shift.

I take the stairs two at a time. My heart is thumping in my chest like a djembe drum.

Mom's bedroom door is closed. Was it closed this morning? I'd been in such a rush I hadn't noticed. Taking a deep breath, I knock just in case she hasn't left for work.

"Mom? I'm back from school."

No answer. I wait a few moments and then, my heart still hammering away inside my ribcage like a woodpecker, I slowly open the door.

"Mom?"

The bed is empty, its cheery red-and-yellow flowered quilt stretched neatly over the mattress.

I walk into the middle of the room. It's so quiet I can hear the rumble of a bus on the road outside and the soft beating of rain against the windowpane. A wave of dizziness sweeps over me and I realize I've been holding my breath for the last few moments.

She isn't here. There's no note. And nothing's been touched. She hasn't come home all day.

## CHAPTER 10

I sit down on the edge of the bed and try not to panic. Where is Mom? Could she have been offered an extra shift? Had she been asked to stay on and work today and said yes because it meant more money? Deep down I know there's no way. She'd never change her plans like that without informing me first. We always let each other know where we'll be and when we'll be back.

I place the palms of my hands against my face, taking refuge for a moment in their dark softness.

Then it comes to me. Her cellphone! Mom bought one yesterday and left the number on a piece of paper on the bulletin board in the kitchen. Why hadn't I thought of that before?

There's a red phone box at the bottom of the road. Grabbing my jacket and the phone number, I open the front door and step outside onto the concrete walkway.

"Oi! Watch out!" A miniature red bike flies past me, its tires just missing my toes. "Get outta the way, lady!"

Twisting his body away from the handlebars, a small boy of about five glares at me. The skin around his mouth and chin is smudged with remnants of what looks like chocolate. I want to wring his neck.

Instead, I turn and hurry down the steps to the side of the building. The cold drizzle is steady rain now. I zip my jacket as I run across the parking lot between our block of flats and the street. Yellow light spills from the streetlamps, throwing jaundiced shadows across my path. A rush of people, their umbrellas held high, pass me as I make my way to the bottom of the hill.

Once inside the phone box, I listen to the angry drumming of the rain while rummaging around the front pocket of my jeans for some change. The wet denim makes it almost impossible to manoeuvre my fingers. I finally retrieve a pound coin. Tucking the phone's receiver between my shoulder and the side of my face, I take out the piece of paper with Mom's number on it and dial.

As soon as it begins ringing, my body relaxes. In a few moments, Mom will pick up and give me a logical explanation for all of this. Three rings. I begin to drum my fingers against the glass in time to the raindrops outside, noticing how quickly my breath is causing the windows of the booth to fog up with condensation. Five rings …

A sharp rapping sound on the glass right beside my head makes me jump. The receiver drops to the floor where it rattles around like a decapitated snake.

Before I can even pick up the phone, the door

flies open and a matted head of grey, woolly hair appears.

"You goin' take all night, Missy?" the man snaps, revealing teeth that look and smell like they've been soaked in urine.

I cover my nose with my hand to keep from retching. He smells like Peaches's litter box would when I forgot to clean it.

"What's the problem? Cat got your pretty tongue?" He leans forward, filling the entire doorway. His eyes slowly crawl up and down the length of my body. Then he raises an eyebrow at me and smirks.

My body freezes in fear. Things happen to girls my age in situations like this. When I was only ten, two girls were abducted in Toronto and killed within a couple of months of each other. One of them was walking from a friend's house in broad daylight. She was only blocks away from her house. Like I am now.

"Are you trying to phone your boyfriend? I've got a nice phone at my flat." He leans in closer. "I'll even let you use it for free."

I look the man in the eye, trying not to vomit. His body odour is now so strong I can taste it. I should shout at him to get other people's attention, but my vocal chords are frozen with fear.

Our eyes lock. His are a reptilian green. The left one is milky.

Suddenly his hand shoots out and clamps onto my wrist, his fingers digging into my bones.

I think about Mom. I can't let this man do anything to me; I can't leave Mom on her own.

"Let go!" I yell. Then I scream as loudly as I can.

The man clamps his free hand over my mouth and wrenches my head back. Pain rushes up my neck into the base of my skull.

"Shut up you little ..."

Before he can finish, I take a deep breath and sink my teeth into the fleshy skin of his palm as hard as I can. His skin tastes bitter and dirty.

Now it's his turn to scream. He snatches his hand away from my face as though he's just been scalded.

I know I have only seconds to make my escape, so I push him as hard as I can directly in the chest, using both arms and throwing my entire body into the movement. He stumbles aside, leaving a small space in the doorway for me to run out.

The fresh air and rain hits my face, giving me an extra burst of energy. I feel adrenaline surging through me, making every cell in my body feel like it's vibrating. I scream again. Several commuters trudging up the sidewalk on the other side of the street stop and look over. A man and women both wearing suits and carrying briefcases hurry across the street toward me.

"Are you all right? What's happening?"

I point toward the man, who is beating a hasty retreat to the bottom of the hill and around the corner. "He tried to grab me!"

"That old geezer there?" the man asks.

Though I'm still shaking, I can't help but notice how cute he is.

"Dirty pervert," the woman says, her lips flattening into an angry grimace.

"I'll be right back. Watch my bag, would you, darling?" Without waiting for his girlfriend's reply, he drops his leather case and takes off running after the man.

His girlfriend watches until he's rounded the corner, her eyes narrowing with concern.

"I wish he wouldn't do these sorts of things. This isn't the safest neighbourhood." She turns back to me. "Are you hurt?"

I shake my head. Though I kind of like the idea of a good-looking guy coming to my rescue, it was obvious his girlfriend isn't in love with this situation. I feel uncomfortable and wish I could sneak away.

"Do you live around here?"

"What? No," I say. The question startles me.

She regards me carefully. "Well, I think Simon and I should get you home and let your mum and dad know what's happened. They'll likely want to ring the police and to put in a report so that man doesn't hurt some other kid."

I feel a flash of annoyance when she calls me a kid, but ignore it. The big issue is her suggestion to take me home. How am I going to get out of this?

"I live with just my mom. And she's at work until six."

Let this woman drop it. Please. If the police find out Mom hasn't been home for over twenty-four hours and that I have no clue where she is, I'll be taken to into care for sure.

"Actually, if you have a cellphone, maybe I could call her right now and have her leave work to meet me at home. It's already five. She wouldn't have to leave that much earlier than usual." I bite my bottom lip, waiting for her response.

"Of course you can borrow my mobile to ring your mum." She begins rummaging around in her purse. "Are you American?" she asks, handing me the phone.

I shake my head as I flip the phone open. "No, Canadian," I reply. "Thanks for this."

I dial Mom's cell number once more. Somewhere deep in the pit of my stomach a small worm of hope unfurls itself as the phone begins to ring again. If something really terrible had happened to Mom, surely her phone wouldn't still be working, would it?

After three rings, I start to talk into the phone. I might be paranoid, but the woman seems to be watching me really closely.

"Hi, Mom. It's me … Susie," I begin. I'm careful to leave a reasonable length of time between speaking. "Something really bad happened today … no, I'm okay … it's just I think it would be good if you came home as soon as possible so I could talk to you about it … This man tried to grab me … no, no really I'm okay. Seriously! Some really nice people came to help me." I flash a wide smile at the woman. "Okay, see you soon … love you too." I press the button to hang up, ending my imaginary conversation.

"She's leaving work right now," I say, handing the phone back.

Simon comes bounding back at that very moment. The woman's attention immediately switches from me to him. Great timing!

"Are you all right? What happened?" she asks, a little more breathlessly than I think is necessary. It's pretty obvious he's okay.

Simon, still breathing heavily, runs a hand through his blond hair and sighs. "Got away, didn't he? Must've slipped onto a train or the Tube. I saw him go into the station. Fast for an old geezer."

"Never mind. I'm glad you didn't catch him. You never know what he might do. Anyway, Susie's going to go with her mum to the police and let them know what happened."

Simon turns to me. "Can we at least walk you home?"

"Thanks, but no thanks. I'm only just up the hill. I'll be okay, really."

"I thought you said you didn't live around here," the woman says with a frown.

Stupid me. I hold my breath, desperately trying to scramble together an explanation.

"God, Mom would kill me if she thought I was telling people I just met on the street where we lived. You know, stranger danger and all that stuff."

The woman opens her mouth to speak, but Simon interjects.

"I understand," he says. "If I had a daughter I wouldn't be able to let her out of my sight the way things are going in this city."

I nod. "Besides, you've already been so great

chasing him away from me and stuff. Thanks so much."

"Just a minute," Simon says, opening his satchel. He pulls out a brown leather wallet. "Here's my card in case the police want to speak to us at all. They'll likely want to."

He hands me a business card. Emblazoned across a red background is a blue and white logo that reads: CHESTNUT ESTATE AGENTS: WHERE YOUR HOME IS OUR HOME. In the bottom is the name SIMON THOMPSON, ESTATE AGENT.

"Take care of yourself, Susie," Simon calls over his shoulder as they cross the street.

"I will," I say, tucking the card into the front pocket of my jeans. I need to keep Simon's contact information safe. After all, there's no telling who I'll have to turn to for help if Mom doesn't show up soon.

# CHAPTER 11

I try to contain my tears as I walk to school the next day. I spent last night alternately sobbing and pressing a cold, wet facecloth against my eyes in a desperate attempt to get rid of the puffiness and red blotches. The last thing I want is for anyone at school to suspect something is wrong — especially teachers.

Mom didn't come home. I lay awake most of the night, listening to distant sirens and the occasional murmur of conversation that floated through the walls of my bedroom from the flat next door. At some point early in the morning my fear and sadness was overtaken by exhaustion and I fell into a fitful sleep.

I think about my situation as I walk. Should I go to the police? There's no doubt now that something serious has happened. Mom might be hurt and lying unconscious in a hospital somewhere, unable to be identified. Maybe she had a head injury or amnesia or something.

I chew on my bottom lip, blinking back tears once more. We've been through so much together and now this. It seems unfair. If I go to the police, they might take me away, even if Mom is found safe. There's no way I'm going to risk that. Not yet.

I stare up at the sky. Once again the day is slate grey, the sky hanging as low as a pregnant cat's belly. The clouds look like they could fall any moment, crushing all the frantic activity happening on the streets below. It feels strange to be going to school, considering that I have no idea where Mom is. But I realize the safest thing to do right now is to act completely normal so that no one suspects anything is wrong.

To say the school day is beginning badly would be a massive understatement. It turns out Ms. Bryans is still absent, but rather than being greeted by the anxious grimace of yet another supply teacher, Mr. Middleton is standing at the front of the classroom as we file in. He's leaning casually against a desk, his arms folded across his chest. The entire class takes their seats and sits silently.

"As all of you are aware, our guest teacher, Ms. Thelwell, was treated in a shameful manner yesterday." He pauses for a moment and slowly scans the room.

"Due to this, today your classes will be covered by Windrush teachers. And, since all of you have seen fit to inconvenience the hard-working staff at this school, I've decided that all of you will serve detention for an hour with me today."

This is met with groans and sucking of teeth. Mr. Middleton's words barely register with me. I don't care. Not now. My eyes are firmly glued to the container sitting on top of the filing cabinet behind Ms. Bryans's desk. It's the charity can she was holding the other day when Jermaine and I were in detention.

There's at least eighty pounds in there. A chart at the front of the room shows how close we are to our goal of raising two hundred pounds to establish a girls' school in Afghanistan. Ms. Bryans must've really been feeling sick if she forgot to hide it away under lock and key before leaving the school. Eighty pounds could keep me eating for at least two weeks and cover the travel costs necessary to search for Mom.

I need to get my hands on that money.

Finding Mom will be like trying to find a contact lens in a sandbox. London is so much bigger and a million times busier than Toronto. The map of the subway looks like a rat's nest of jumbled-up wires, with all the different colours criss-crossing each other.

Having to search London by myself to try and find Mom terrifies me. I have no idea where to even start. However, the thought of never seeing her again scares me even more. I have to get that money before someone else in the class gets the same idea.

Morning classes pass excruciatingly slowly. I try to concentrate on the work in front of me, but competing waves of fatigue and worry make it too difficult. By the time the lunch bell rings though, I'm ready. I'm getting that money over the next hour. If Ms. Bryans returns tomorrow, there might not be another chance.

First, I need to get my lunch from the cafeteria. That way at least a few people will see me doing my usual thing at lunch. I purchase a salad and some curried chicken with rice and go sit with Savitri and Keisha.

"Hey, girl. We were just discussing what a bloody cow Ms. Thompson was to us today," Savitri says. "Didn't she give us enough work to last a week?"

I can't actually remember much about the work Ms. Thompson, who was usually our physical education teacher, had assigned. Every teacher that covered our class this morning took their frustration out on us.

"And she didn't have to be such a bitch," Savitri adds, spooning curry into her mouth. "I asked her if I could go to the toilet and she said no! What if I had to change a tampon or something?"

Keisha laughs. "I wish that had've happened. Then if she said no and you'd had an accident, we could've gotten her sacked for sure!"

"Thanks," Savitri says, narrowing her eyes at Keisha. "Then I would've died of embarrassment as well."

I nod in agreement. There aren't many worse things that could happen to a girl in front of the whole class.

"Don't be stupid. I don't actually wish that happened to you. Besides," says Keisha, taking a sip of her Coke, "it really isn't right that your whole class is getting punished for just a few twats like Rodney. I wish Mr. Middleton would just punish the people involved."

As we talk, I aimlessly move the mound of congealing curry and rice around on my plate and try to think of an excuse to leave the table without Keisha and Savitri thinking I'm ditching them. After all, it feels good to be making some friends at Windrush, especially considering the mess my life is in at the moment.

"Hey, I hate to cut things short, but I need to go and do a few things before class starts," I say, glancing at my watch.

"What's popping?" Keisha asks.

"I've got to get a few things for my mom. She's busy with work today."

"Are you going to Tesco?" Savitri asks. "If you are, I'll come with you. I'm starving. I hate the rubbish they try to pass off on us as food here. Much rather a bag of crisps."

"Great," I reply. "I just need to get something from my locker first." I pause for a second. "Money. I have to get my money."

"You're awfully nice to go to the shops for your mum, Edie," Keisha says as she reaches for Savitri's discarded plate. "Miss Posh here," she adds, pointing her fork toward Savitri, "seems to think any school dinner that's not cooked by Jamie bloody Oliver himself isn't good enough for her."

Savitri waves a dismissive hand at Keisha. I pick up my tray and get up from the table.

"Be back in a minute," I say.

"You best be quick about it, Edie!" Savitri replies. "Middleton will have our heads if we're late for any classes today!"

I walk quickly along the hallway toward the classroom. There's a strict rule at Windrush banning students from being in the halls over lunch without a pass from a teacher. I hope the door has been left unlocked. If Ms. Thompson locked it at lunch dismissal, then I'll have to kiss that money goodbye. But I don't want to think about that because it means no money to search for Mom or to buy food when the groceries left at home run out.

I grab the metal doorknob, hold my breath, and turn it firmly to the right. It's unlocked.

Stepping inside, I close the door carefully behind me and walk over to the filing cabinet. The tin of money is still there. I reach up, grab it, and shove it into my knapsack.

"Oi! What are you mucking about in here for, eh?"

I swing around, my heart pounding in my ears.

Jermaine Lewis is leaning against the door, arms folded across the front of his black hoodie. He smirks at me, clearly pleased he's caught me so off-guard.

"Nothing," I stammer. "I thought I left something in here."

"Really? Where's your hall pass, then?"

I pause. It hits me that I'm alone in a closed classroom with someone who is supposedly a murderer. And no one knows I'm here.

"Where's yours?" I ask. "And who died and made you hall monitor, anyway?"

Jermaine laughs. The way he's looking at me makes my face flush.

He opens his right palm, revealing a hall pass.

"You're funny," he replies. "Did you find what you came for?"

"What?"

"The thing you forgot that you needed to come back to class for? Did you get it?"

"Oh. Yeah, I did. It was just some book … I've got to go." My tongue is working faster than my brain. What a stupid thing to say.

Cheeks burning, I walk past Jermaine and into the hall. Once I'm outside the school, a rush of adrenaline floods my body. I have the money. Now the real challenge begins. Now I need to find Mom.

## CHAPTER 12

I try not to be too hopeful as I walk into the flat, but I can't help visualizing Mom waiting on the couch for me to come home with some crazy story to explain her disappearance. I'd listen. We'd laugh. And then Mom would make dinner.

That doesn't happen.

Instead, I walk in, drop my knapsack, and listen. The flat is silent. The steady ticking of the wall clock in the kitchen beats in time with my heart. I wait a few more seconds, standing completely still like a jungle animal stalking its prey. Listening. Waiting.

Then I go upstairs. She hasn't been back. It's obvious. As I walk into my mother's room, my composure shatters. I kick the door shut behind me, rip the duvet off the bed, and scream.

My rage frightens me. I'm so angry with Mom for disappearing and at *him* for causing my life to turn out this way. The next target for my frustration is an assortment of cosmetics, various papers, and a vase of tulips on top of Mom's dresser. With one violent sweep of my arm, I send the entire mess flying. A container of taupe eyeshadow smashes against the wall, leaving a smear of flesh-coloured powder behind. The broken stalks of the tulips lie on the floor surrounded by a pool of water. But I don't care.

Finally my anger gives way to sadness and I collapse in tears, pulling the duvet around me. I lay down on Mom's bed and rock back and forth, trying to ward off the dampness that never seems to subside in this place. I hate London. It's a cold, damp, and miserable place and I'm completely alone.

There's no one in the city I can contact to help me. I flirt briefly with the thought of calling Janice, but don't want to worry her. Besides, it's not like she can stop her whole life in Canada and fly over here to help me look for Mom. And Mom has no family left, aside from a half-sister who lives in Ireland. I've only met her a couple of times when I was much younger. Mom's father and stepmother died in a car accident two years before I was born. We haven't had much contact with any family since we went on the run. I think Mom is kind of ashamed of how things turned out. Still, she must have kept Aunt Siobhan's number somewhere. If I don't find out what happened to Mom in the next few days, I'll try to contact her.

The next morning I wake up feeling tired but hopeful. It's Friday, which means I can spend the weekend searching for Mom without anyone getting suspicious. By not missing any school, no one will think anything is wrong. Besides, I'm now eighty-one pounds richer thanks to the charity fund. I figure that will give me enough money to live on for at least a month if I'm super careful. Last night I walked to Sainsbury's and stocked up on Pot Noodle, milk, apples, and cereal. Having a full stomach makes me feel stronger and more able to face things.

On the way to class I run into Keisha coming out of the one of the shops on the main street near school. A sign taped to the door reads: NO MORE THAN THREE SCHOOLCHILDREN AT ANY TIME. There's at least a dozen students from Windrush crammed in there, though, some of them rummaging through magazines, others hanging around the chocolate bar racks.

"All right, Edie?" Keisha asks, grinning widely as the falls into step with me. "Fancy some?" She offers up part of a Jamaican patty.

I wonder if she can tell something is wrong with me.

"No thanks. I had a huge breakfast."

"God! Aren't you bloody lucky! I never have time to eat at home." She stuffs a corner of the yellow pastry into her mouth. "I've got four little brothers and sisters to get ready for school and then I have to walk them there before I even get to think about me."

"Why do you have to get your brothers and sisters ready?" I ask. "Does your Mom go to work early?" Though I'm afraid Keisha will think I'm being too nosy, I ache to confide in someone about my own situation. Maybe if she's being left alone and responsible for her younger siblings, she might not think it's all that bad that Mom leaves me alone all night to go to work.

Keisha snorts through a mouthful of yellow pastry. "Edie, my mum would get sacked the first day she even tried to be at a real job!" She rolls her eyes. "I left her on the sofa this morning with her second favourite thing in the world — an empty bottle of Appleton's."

"What's her first?" I ask.

Keisha laughs. "A full bottle of Appleton's rum!"

I decide not to tell Keisha about Mom. Suddenly I feel sick and desperately want to change the subject. Mom is a great parent. She's taken care of me during the worst situations. I always came first. I don't want Keisha thinking my mom is anything like hers.

As we approach the school gates, Imogen comes running up to us.

"Have you heard?" she asks breathlessly. "Ms. Bryans and Mr. Middleton are raging mad! Somebody nicked the charity money yesterday!"

It's the first time I've seen any colour in her pale cheeks. Imogen finishes speaking and begins scratching distractedly at a line of raw, sore-looking pimples that run in a crooked ridge across her forehead.

"You're joking!" I say, hoping I sound sincerely shocked.

"God, I'm not surprised," Keisha snorts. "That money was practically asking to be nicked. I would've taken it myself except I don't need to. My mum gives me loads of pocket money every week."

"Our class is never going to be allowed to go to the disco now for sure!" Imogen sighs.

"Were you planning on going then?" Keisha asks, a smirk dancing on her lips. "Did you have a date all lined up?"

Imogen scratches at her forehead again. She lowers her eyes away from Keisha's gaze. "I dunno. But even if I wasn't, I still don't want our whole class to be banned from everything nice."

"I agree," I say. I don't like Keisha's attitude. Despite her weirdness, Imogen is harmless and I hate seeing people get bullied. Bullies remind me too much of *him*. "We've had nothing but lectures for days now and I bet you today's going to be the worst. If I'd known England was going to be like this, I'd have stayed away."

"Bloody hell, Edie!" Keisha laughs. "This place is absolute rubbish! You should've known to stay away, full stop!"

I turns out I wasn't wrong about the lecture. Mr. Middleton is waiting at the front of the class again. This time Ms. Bryans stands beside him, mimicking his stern stance, both of them with their arms crossed firmly over their chests.

As soon as we've taken our seats and are quietly reading novels or finishing homework assignments, Mr. Middleton strides over to the door and shuts it with a bang that is as sharp as a gunshot. Several students jump in their seats. I swear I see Ms. Bryans smile. Just for a second.

"I need everything off your desks and your

attention firmly up here," Mr. Middleton begins. He waits until everyone is watching him.

"I regret having to say this, but the situation with this homeroom has gone from bad to worse," he says, shaking his head at us to reinforce the point. "As a class you are representing Windrush School very poorly. We already have a tenuous — to say the least — reputation in the borough. I'd expect all of you to behave with even more diligence because of that. Now, I'm not saying all of you were involved in the goings on of late, but, as a class, you are a team."

I dig my fingernails into the fleshy pad of my palm, distracting myself with the pain. Mr. Middleton is so wrong. Did he really forget what it's like to be a teenager? We're hardly a team. It's more like survival of the fittest. Not a day goes by where someone isn't bullied, whether online or in person.

"We strongly suspect," Ms. Bryans says, "that the culprit took the money during the lunch hour yesterday. According to Ms. Thompson that money was — without question — still on the filing cabinet when she left the room."

Mr. Middleton nods. "However, Mr. Ravi did not see the tin the following period when he came to teach your first afternoon class."

"That's because he was reading a newspaper the whole time," someone mutters.

Ms. Bryans looks sharply in the direction of the comment. A tiny blue vein pulses above her left temple.

"What we are saying," she interjects, "is that it is almost certain that the money was taken during yesterday's lunch. We also have several witnesses who saw a student from this homeroom coming out of the class during the lunch break without permission."

The words hit me like a sack of bricks. Suddenly the room is too bright and the buzzing sound of the lights fills my ears. Somebody saw me. For a moment I'm afraid I might vomit or faint, or possibly both. The school will phone home if I'm caught. They'll want to talk to Mom. Then everything will fall apart. I'll end up in care for sure.

"Now, of course we're not *accusing* anyone," Mr. Middleton breaks in, shooting Ms. Bryans a warning look. "But I do expect to see that particular individual in my office by the end of the day, as it would be of benefit if the student volunteered his side of the story before being approached by me."

Mr. Middleton pauses for a moment. Some students shoot accusatory glances at each other.

He clears his throat loudly. "Furthermore if this student chooses to do the right thing, it will most certainly help me make a decision as to whether or not this class will be attending the school disco next week."

I'm stunned. *His side of the story.* That's Mr. Middleton just said. Wasn't it? Maybe they don't suspect me at all. Have I gotten away with stealing the charity fund? Or are they just trying to see if I have the guts to confess my crime?

## CHAPTER 13

When the bell rings at the end of the day, I feel triumphant. I can't help but smile as I walk out the school doors. Mr. Middleton hasn't spoken to me. In fact, he passed me in the hall without so much as a glance while I was gathering my books for history class. I don't know who they think is behind the money's disappearance and really don't care. Nothing matters now except finding Mom.

I turn down a laneway. It's a shortcut home that I've discovered. A fine mist of rain begins to fall. Cold fingers of wind claw at the thin jacket I'm wearing. Shivering, I cross my arms in front of my chest in an attempt to keep warm.

"What the bloody hell do you think you're playing at?"

I don't even have time to react before being pushed violently from behind and up against the brick wall. I cry out as the brick scrapes my cheek. At the sound of my cry, the hold on me loosens and I'm able to turn and step away from the wall.

Jermaine stands in front of me, his dark eyes

watching me intensely. His rage is so palpable I can almost taste it. My first instinct is to get away from that anger. But with Jermaine in front of me and the brick wall at my back, there is nowhere to run.

"What are you talking about?" I ask. My voice is barely a whisper. I hate myself for being so scared, but all I can think about was how Jermaine supposedly killed a bunch of kids, including his own brother, and somehow got away with it. That's everyone says; *it was clear he'd done it, but some stupid judge let him off.*

Jermaine kisses his teeth loudly. "What am I on about?" He takes two steps toward me and bends down so that his face is only millimetres away from mine. I can feel the heat radiating from his skin. "I'm talking about the money I was just suspended for nicking."

"I still don't know what you're talking about," I reply, trying to keep my voice even. I suddenly have to go to the bathroom badly. "Ms. Bryans said they found out who took that money. That's all I know."

Jermaine takes a step backward and laughs. His breath turns into little clouds of white vapour as it hits the damp air.

"All right, then. Let's walk through yesterday. You just happened to be in the class at lunch without a hall pass, right?"

"Yeah. So, what's your point?" I ask.

"You're telling me it was just a coincidence that you were in there when the money disappeared?"

"You heard what they said. It was a male student who took the money."

"No, what they said was that people saw a student coming out of our classroom yesterday during lunch. What they didn't bother saying was that they were talking about me. Funny thing is, I had a hall pass. And you saw it. Mr. Ravi gave it to me. But what's even more funny is that when Ravi was asked about it, he denied ever giving me a hall pass."

'Well, I can vouch for you," I interject. "I can tell them that I saw your hall pass."

Jermaine smirks. "And what'll you do when they ask where *your* pass was?"

He's right. I feel badly that he's being punished for my crime, but there's no way I'll confess to the school administration about taking that money.

I glance at Jermaine again. His red cotton hoodie is soaked, he has no jacket on, and he still looks angry. I owe him some sort of explanation. I take a deep breath.

"I had to take that money," I blurt out. "My mom hasn't been home for more than twenty-four hours. I took the money so I can find her. I need it for transportation. And to get food ... so I can eat." Though I hadn't really meant to tell Jermaine everything, I feel a sense of relief. The secret finally isn't just mine.

He regards me carefully like he's trying to decide whether or not I'm telling the truth.

"Are you having me on?" he finally asks.

"No ..."

"Did Keisha and Savitri put you up to this?"

"What?" I ask, taken aback.

"You heard me. Are you taking the piss? Is it a laugh for you?"

I shake my head. "I don't know what you mean."

"Getting me in trouble is what I mean. Is it funny to all of you?"

The anger is back, resonating off him in waves. It was evident Jermaine didn't believe my explanation for stealing the money.

"No, I swear. Keisha and Savitri don't even know I took the money."

"And I'm supposed to believe a thief?"

It's raining harder. Drops of water ricochet off the pavement. Even they seem full of rage.

"I'm sorry," I stammer. "But I can't tell anyone I took that money. Especially not Mr. Middleton. At least not yet."

Jermaine glares at me. "You have no idea what you've done," he says, his voice low. "Stay away from me. And best hope I stay away from you."

He turns and walks away without so much as a glance back at me. I stand for a moment in the rain watching him, not wanting to turn my back until I know he's a safe distance away. Then I begin to run.

# CHAPTER 14

I don't stop running until I'm back at the flat. By the time I reach the parking lot in front of the building, my lungs feel as though they've been doused in gasoline and set on fire. My hair sticks in soaking strands to my cheeks and neck. I'm a mess.

As I walk onto the landing outside the flat, I'm startled to see a man and a woman knocking on our door. They're both wearing yellow vests. I've seen police officers around their station in the centre of Lewisham just opposite the Pizza Hut, but these uniforms aren't quite the same. I slow my pace and try to steady my breathing.

The man looks up as I approach. "Hello there," he says, flashing me a goofy grin that reveals teeth in bad need of a visit to a dentist's office. "Do you live here?"

I pause. But just for a moment.

"In this building? Yeah." My heart's thumping so hard I'm sure they can see it beating through my jacket.

"Do you live at this flat?" he asks, nodding at our door.

"No," I reply. "I live two doors down."

They exchange a knowing glance. Every muscle in my body tenses.

"That's too bad. We're hoping to speak to the residents of this flat," the woman says, nodding her head toward our door. "Maybe you know them?" She raises an eyebrow questioningly at me.

I shrug. "Nope. Sorry. I can't help you." I walk past the two of them, pretending to head toward one of the flats farther along the concrete walkway.

"That's so curious," the man replies from behind me. "Because the girl who supposedly lives here is just about your age and from Canada."

Before the words are out of his mouth I begin to run, my legs propelling me toward the staircase at the end of the walkway.

Running footsteps fall in time with mine, but I don't dare turn around. That would only slow me down. The man is tall and lean and I need every advantage I can get.

I reach the stairs and hurl myself down them two at a time, praying I won't lose my footing. The cold metal of the railing slides under my palm. It's the only thing keeping me from falling headfirst down the steps.

"Wait!" the man shouts. My heart jumps. He's so near it sounds like he's almost yelling in my ear. "Please stop! We just want to have a word with you."

*Screw you*, I think. They're some sort of police,

maybe not like the ones I see walking around the neighbourhood by the school or in their little white cop cars, but close enough. Close enough that there's no way I'm going to stop. They stick together. I know that all too well. And it doesn't matter if you're police in a different country. If they're looking for me then I can bet Dad's found us after all. And he likely found Mom first.

I leap from the staircase, leaving the final four steps untouched. My shoes hit the asphalt of the parking lot with a thud, sending a sharp pain through my right ankle like a bolt of lightning. This momentarily throws me off-balance, but there's no time to stop.

Lungs burning, I run down the street, retracing my earlier route. Jermaine's warning is a distant memory. Little did he know some schoolyard threat isn't going to scare me. I'm used to dealing with fear.

I doubt the man will chase me once I am off our housing estate, but I'm not taking any chances and continue running to the bottom of the hill and across the main street toward the train station. I enter the front doors, sprint past a long line of people waiting to buy tickets, bound down the nearest set of stairs, and dash onto the platform just as a train is approaching. A small crowd of soon-to-be passengers stand waiting. Some are hastily taking the last drags off cigarettes while others keep their faces firmly buried in a book or newspaper. I try to blend in even though I must look like I've just run a marathon with werewolves chasing me.

*"The train approaching Platform Two is a Connex-Southeastern service calling at St. John's, Blackheath ..."*

The rest of the announcement fades from my consciousness the second I notice two yellow flashes. The officers are standing at the top of the stairs.

They followed me! I'm trapped with nowhere to go but onto the train. And not only do I not have a ticket; I have absolutely no idea where this train is going. The destinations announced a few moments ago might as well have been in China.

The doors to the train slide open and a surge of city workers in their suits pour out like water from a burst dam. I glance toward the staircase again and that's when the man points at me. Within seconds, they're both running down the stairs. Sweat breaks out on my forehead.

I have no choice. I'm getting on that train.

Pushing my way forward, I hurry on. Every seat is taken and standing room means jamming your body against the other passengers around you. Gross.

*Mind the doors, the doors are closing ...*

I look out the window. They're steps away from the door, having been slowed down by the crowd of commuters trying to make their way up the stairs, out of the station and home. The man is shouting something as he claws his way to the door.

Then there's a sudden lurch and the fat man stuffing his face full of chips beside me loses his balance for a moment and falls forward, putting one of his greasy paws on my shoulder to steady himself.

"Sorry," he wheezes. Though his onion breath makes me want to puke, I don't care. We pull away from the station, leaving the man and woman on the platform, staring in frustration as the train leaves New Cross Gate, taking me with it.

## CHAPTER 15

The train's first stop is Blackheath and I decide to get off. I don't want to go too far, but I need to be sure that the two officers will not be able to find me easily. That means getting as far away from the station as I can as quickly as possible.

Though it's only a five-minute train ride away, Blackheath might as well be on another planet; it is so different from New Cross. No more taxi stands with chipped signs. The Caribbean food takeout shops and rundown hairdressers have disappeared as well. Instead, as I turn down the street and walk away from the station, I pass boutiques full of designer clothes, fancy food stores, and a Starbucks. Hunger strikes me like a boxer's fist as I peer inside and see people eating. I feel around in my jacket pocket and pull out a five-pound note and a handful of change.

It's weird being in a Starbucks in England. Pretty much everything is the same as in Canada. Rumi and I used to go to the Starbucks near George

Brown College, pretend we were students there, and drink caramel macchiatos. Thinking about the future and daydreaming about what we'd be doing as college or university students made real life easier sometimes.

"Can I get a grande caramel macchiato and a croissant, please?" I ask the girl behind the counter.

"Whipped cream?"

I smile. "Of course."

She smiles back at me as she grabs a cup. "Takeaway or eat in?"

I look outside. The sky is clearing and the rain has finally stopped, leaving the sidewalks awash with tiny puddles that glisten under the streetlamps. I want to get back to the flat before it gets very late. Especially since I really have no idea where I am.

"To go. I mean, takeaway."

"Are you just visiting?" she asks. A generous helping of fluffy white cream is spooned on top of my drink.

"Nope. I live nearby." Even though I know this Starbucks chick is completely harmless, the question still makes me jumpy. I can't shake the fear that I might still be followed or, worse yet, that somehow Dad has managed to get everyone in London searching for me.

Outside, the cold air hits me like a slap. The warmth from the cup soothes my bare hands as I continue to walk up the street until I come to a fork in the road. I follow the right side, emerging a few minutes later onto a massive expanse of flat, green land. In the distance, headlights from a traffic jam litter the night like tiny fireflies.

I walk along, pulling my jacket up as far as I can to try to cover my neck and block out the biting wind. Though I can't be that far from New Cross, I have no idea what direction to walk in to get back. Being alone on a dark field makes me want to scream my skin inside out, but I know I need to stay calm. I'm probably a thousand times safer right now than I've ever been walking around Regent after dark and I'd done that loads of times. Yet I can't shake the fear that Dad knows where I am and that it's just a matter of time before he catches up to me.

After what seems like ages, I reach the road and stand, my face illuminated by the headlights of the cars, trying to figure out which way to walk. Though I can see the shadows of a few houses away to my left and across the road, the area is strangely deserted. It's hard to believe I'm still in London. I look over my shoulder. The lights of Blackheath twinkle behind me. I've never felt so alone in my entire life.

Eventually I find a 171 bus that is heading back to New Cross. I don't know what to expect back at the flat. Part of me wonders if maybe I was wrong about the man and woman. Maybe they have nothing to do with him; perhaps someone ratted me out and they were sent from the school to inform Mom about the missing money. Except Mom is missing. And deep down I believe the visit happening so soon after Mom disappearing isn't a coincidence.

I get off the bus and take a different route back to the flat just in case anyone is watching. Not going back to the flat isn't an option unless I want to spend the night on the streets.

Every step I take seems to echo along the pavement. I can't shake the feeling that I'm being watched and stop several times like a spy from some kid's cartoon to hide behind a tree, staying still for several minutes to see if anyone emerges from the shadows to search me out.

I make it to our building and hurry quickly along the concrete walkway toward the stairwell.

A hooded shadow emerges from behind one of the parked cars as I pass. Every muscle in my body stops and tenses. The sound of my heart pounding fills my ears.

"About time. Freezing my balls off out here."

Jermaine pulls back his hood, leans against the car, and regards me carefully. What does he want? Suddenly I'm afraid. I thought his threat was empty. Clearly I was wrong.

"Are you some kind of psycho stalker?" I snap, jabbing my index finger at him. "How did you know I lived here?"

"I followed you after school." He doesn't seem angry anymore. "Wanted to see if you were lying about your mum."

"Why would I lie about my mom disappearing? Does that seem like a funny joke to you?" Tears well up in my eyes just talking about it. I'm exhausted and cold from walking around in the damp all evening.

"Naw. But I've taken the fall for you in a big way and I need this sorted."

"Well, I have to find my mom first. Then I promise I'll tell everyone that I took the money. I'll even take an ad out in the paper," I quip.

"Yeah that's brilliant," Jermaine replies. "While you're being all smart about this, I'll be taken into care."

I open my mouth, but nothing comes out.

"That's right. My mum was told if I got into any more trouble they were going to take me away from her. And the school calling about the money and me being suspended is going to be just the reason they need to do it."

I close my eyes for a moment. I took that money so that no one would know Mom was gone; so the school wouldn't call Children's Aid or whatever they called it here. Because I did that, someone else is about to be taken away from his mom. Still, I have to think of Mom and me first. It's the only way to survive. If I begin caring too much about what's happening with others, it will only make things harder.

"I'm sorry," I say. I figure saying it might make him lay off. Anyway, I can't help him unless I find out what's happened to Mom.

Jermaine looks slightly unconvinced. He crosses his arms against his chest. "So, does your mum do this often? Take off?"

My eyes widen. "No! Of course not. This has never happened before. She works nights in the city and just …" I trail off for a moment, not trusting myself to speak without crying and I'm not going to cry in front of him. "She just didn't come home the other morning."

Jermaine lets out a low whistle. "Does she do something dodgy like being a prostitute?"

"Screw you," I say bitterly. I push past him and run to the stairwell.

"Hey! It was just a question. Don't get angry." Jermaine is beside me within seconds. He grabs my elbow. I snatch my arm back and wheel around.

"Don't touch me," I snap.

"Sorry," he says, holding his hands up as if he's surrendering to me. "I just don't think you should go up there alone. I saw community police chasing you today. What's up with that?"

So that's who they were.

I shake my head. "I have no idea."

"Maybe they have some information about your mum."

"I bet they do," I say bitterly. "But I wasn't sticking around to find out."

Jermaine raises an eyebrow at me, but doesn't probe further. "If you need to find your mum before you'll come clean about the charity money, I better help you."

"Why should I trust you to help me?' I ask. Hunger, fatigue, and cold are combining to make me super-irritable.

"Well, let's see … maybe because I'm the only one that knows you nicked that money. And I also know your mum isn't anywhere around and that no one is looking after you right now."

He has me there. I let the secret out and have no one to blame for that but myself. Besides, Jermaine seems okay from what I can tell. He doesn't appear to be the psycho that Savitri and Keisha make him out to be. At least I hope he isn't.

"Fine," I say. "You can walk me to the door and then come by tomorrow morning. But make it early. I need to begin looking for Mom a.s.a.p."

"Any idea where to start?" Jermaine asks. We begin walking up the stairs. It's so cold that little clouds of smoky vapour hit the air in front of us as we talk.

I pause.

"No. But I'll figure that out tonight. You just show tomorrow at nine o'clock."

Jermaine smiles. "We'll find her, Edie."

I turn and look him in the eye. "I hope you really believe that," I say. "Because there is no other choice."

# CHAPTER 16

Jermaine brought up a good point; I need a plan. In the avalanche of panic I've felt following Mom's disappearance, I haven't even thought to search the flat for clues to her whereabouts.

And it ends up being so easy. In the drawer of her bedside table, I find Mom's brown leather agenda. Inside there's a hastily jotted note about an interview on January 6. The address is scrawled in her handwriting: *Corporate Cleaners, 31b White Horse Road, Limehouse E1.*

I sit down on the side of the bed and stare at the notes in the agenda. Mom always uses blue ink in her agenda. I trace the words with my index finger, savouring the way each letter is formed. These words are a link to her. A wet blotch falls onto the page and my vision blurs. I close the book.

Enough. There's no time to sit and cry. After what happened today with the community police officers stalking me outside the flat, I'm positive Mom's in trouble. Serious trouble. And likely I'm in it up to my neck as well. I need to be ready for tomorrow.

I put the book into my bag along with one of my favourite photos of Mom, wash up, and climb into bed. Pulling the covers up to my chin, I look out the window. London lights up the night sky. A light blinking on and off at the top of one of the tall buildings across the river catches my eye. I wonder if it is used to warn low-flying planes like the one that Mom and I travelled here on. The thought of our journey makes me think of all the times we've picked up and moved. Before this move, the farthest we'd fled was from Toronto to Vancouver and back.

Suddenly I realize how tired I am of running. And that's when I decide there's no way I'll be scared into running again. I'm older now. This time I'm ready to fight.

Even though I hardly slept, I get up at seven to give myself time to look decent. After all, I'm heading into London. And I'm going with Jermaine. I try to go for the natural look with my makeup, except I need shovel-loads of concealer under my eyes to cover the raccoon circles I've got from not really sleeping since Mom disappeared.

And, just like he promised, Jermaine shows up at exactly nine o'clock.

"Ready?" he asks, leaning against the doorframe.

"Let me just run upstairs and grab a heavier

jacket," I say, glancing up at the grey blanket of sky. Little rows of goosebumps emerge on my lower arms. "God, it feels colder here than in Canada. Come on in." Jermaine walks past me into the narrow hallway. I close the door and dash up the stairs, hoping the jeans I'm wearing don't make my bum look wide.

"Make yourself comfortable!" I shout back over my shoulder.

Inside my bedroom, I pause for a moment before opening the mirrored door of my wardrobe. Over the last couple of years my appearance has changed so rapidly, I sometimes barely recognize myself. The roundness of my face is completely gone, replaced by angles and protruding cheekbones. My hair is a darker, deeper chestnut colour now and my body is elongated and filled out. Everywhere there are curves that just three years ago were non-existent.

I tilt my head, noting how my red cotton sweater pulls tightly across my breasts. It looks good, other than the fact that the sleeves are slightly too short so I push them up my forearms. I reach into the pocket of my jeans, take out a pot of deep red gloss and coat my lips so that they shine. Running a hand through my hair, I stand back and take one last, approving glance at my reflection, put on my black winter jacket, and hurry downstairs.

"Where are we?" I ask as we get off the bus. "That was one of the shortest bus rides of my life." We're standing at a busy intersection. The heavy smell of car exhaust invades my nostrils.

"Deptford Bridge. You said the address your mum wrote down for work was in Limehouse, yeah?"

I flip back through the agenda. "Yep, Limehouse."

"We'll take the Docklands there," he says, crossing the street.

I follow him, realizing just how lucky I am to have Jermaine helping me. I wouldn't have the faintest clue about how to get around London without him. Over the past twenty-four hours I began to realize the probability of something really unpleasant having happened to Mom was increasing. I still hoped that there'd been some sort of freak accident and that she was lying in the hospital somewhere, unconscious or suffering from a temporary loss of memory.

"You have an Oyster card?" Jermaine asks.

I snap back to the present. "No," I reply. "What's that?"

"You'll need one to travel around. Too late to go to the shop so we'll grab a Travelcard for today." He stops in front of the ticket machine at the bottom of a flight of concrete stairs. A train rumbles overhead.

"Oh," I open my bag and rummage around for my wallet. I hand him some of the money from the charity fund.

After purchasing a card, Jermaine bounds up the long set of stairs with me following, trying to keep up as best I can. A train is approaching the platform as we reach the top of the steps. Jermaine runs to the first car, his long legs propelling him forward effortlessly, and punches the button on the side of the carriage with a closed fist. He slips inside as soon as the doors open.

We take seats at the very front of the train. Despite my worry about Mom, I can't help feel an electric current of excitement dance up my spine as the train pulls away from the platform and begins slipping toward Greenwich.

"You ever been on this ride?" Jermaine asks.

"No. I haven't actually been in London very long," I admit.

He glances at me. "When did you get here?"

"Just a day or two before school started after the break. Our move was kind of … rushed." An image of Peaches curled up at the foot of my bed jumps into my mind. *Rushed*. What an understatement.

We sit in silence for a few minutes after that. I can feel Jermaine wanting to ask me more. It's one of the things I like about him; he can tell I'm holding back information about my situation but isn't nosy enough to ask about it.

I look around at the people on the train. Like Toronto, the passengers are from all the corners of the world. A beautiful Muslim woman sits with her little boy on the seats across from us, a silver-and-blue hijab thrown loosely over her head, allowing wisps of dark hair as shiny as silk threads to peek out from either side of the fabric. The little boy, who looks like he's around four or five, claps his hands together and whoops raucously as our train swoops underground into darkness.

I smile at the little boy. The mom and her son remind me of Regent Park. Most of my friends, including Rume, were Muslim. I loved being invited to iftar at her house during Ramadan. Somehow, even though we were all different in the Park, it always seemed like everyone was accepted and part of something bigger. I never really knew what being lonely or feeling left out meant while I lived there. I definitely know what it feels like now.

"You know what the *Cutty Sark* is?" Jermaine asks me as the train makes its first stop.

I shake my head.

"It's one of the most famous ships in the world. It's a clipper; it was used as a tea ship. I'll take you to see it after we find your mum."

As the doors close and the train lurches away from the station, I smile to myself. I like the way Jermaine said he'd take me to see the ship. Though I don't care about old ships, I have a feeling I'll find this one a lot more interesting with Jermaine showing me it. I can't understand why the teachers at Windrush don't notice how smart he is. It's like they've already written him off and no amount of evidence showing them they're wrong will ever change their minds.

"We're under the river now," Jermaine says, interrupting my thoughts. "We'll be on the north side in just a few moments.

"Really?" I think about how crazy it is to be zipping along in a train through a little tunnel under massive amounts of water. Just one random crack and all that water could come crashing down on us. So many random events change people's lives in just the blink of an eye. Earthquakes, cars losing control, planes crashing … and people going to work and disappearing into thin air. I grimace. Somehow I always manage to think of the worst-case scenarios for everything.

"North side of the Thames now," Jermaine says. The train pulls up alongside a platform. I glance out the window, watching passengers disembark.

"Why do the teachers give you such a hard time at school?" I ask.

He doesn't answer for a moment and I immediately regret having said anything. If I could, I'd stuff my whole size-seven shoe down my throat until it came out my bum to be able to take the question back.

"Sorry. It's none of my business."

Jermaine shrugs. "It's okay … I don't know why they do it. 'Cos they're all wankers and twats?" he says, giving me a lopsided grin.

"Seriously. I mean I hate it when teachers think they know everything about me. They don't know anything."

He nods. "You got that right."

We sit in silence for a few moments. I want desperately to ask him what he's thinking, but that would make me a big, fat cliché of a girl, so I don't.

I glance over at the platform. "Mudchute? Is that seriously the name of the station?"

Jermaine laughs. "Yeah. What of it? I'm sure you have some funny underground station names in Canada."

I think for a minute. "There's Broadview. I don't know why, but I that always struck me as a strange subway stop name."

"Probably some bloke named it after his girl," he replies.

I shoot him a puzzled look.

"You know … he was probably like, 'Mhmmm, girl. I like your booty. That's one *broad* view.'"

I punch him in the arm. "Pig."

He reaches over and grabs me around the neck, putting me in a mock headlock.

"Take it back or beg for mercy."

The fabric of his sweater feels soft and inviting against my cheek and I inhale deeply, taking in the faint smell of lemons and wool. I don't want to take it back because that means he'll let go.

"Did you just smell me?" he asks.

I wiggle out of his grasp and bolt over to my seat, sitting up as straight as my back will allow. My face is hot. *Don't blush, you fool*, I think to myself, willing the blood in my face to somehow instantaneously drain to my feet.

"No! Are you sick? Why would I go around smelling *you*?"

He laughs. "My mum is always saying to me, Boy, you must be smelling yourself."

"What does that mean?"

"That I'm about to get my head cuffed." He

stops laughing and his eyes darken. "She's not well. She hardly notices anything I do right now."

I don't know how to reply. An uncomfortable silence spreads between us as the train surfaces out from the tunnel and into the light again.

## CHAPTER 17

Salty sea air, the faint smell of dead fish and exhaust fumes all cling to the air as we walk down the stairs at Limehouse station.

"Where now?" Jermaine asks.

I pause. "I have no idea," I admit. "The place is on White Horse Road."

We walk onto a bustling street. This place is a way nicer version of London than New Cross. Modern condo buildings intermingle with well-kept, older brick houses that show off carefully tended flower-boxes and brightly painted doors.

"Hold on," Jermaine says, stopping and removing the straps of his knapsack from his back. He unzips it and pulls out a book.

"If you haven't been in London long, you need to get one of these." He holds up a white-jacketed book. *A–Z London* is written across the front cover. It turns out to be a novel-sized map book.

After finding the direction we need to go in to find the cleaning company, we begin walking with purpose. My stomach feels like a wet towel that's twisted into tight knots. This all seems like such a shot in the dark. After all, I can't even be sure Mom made it to work at all on her first day.

Jermaine gives a low whistle. "Blimey, this is a bit of nice."

I look at the building we've stopped in front of. Cristina's Cleaning Company is located above a quaint flower shop. Displays of almost every colour and shape of flower imaginable are set out in shining, silver metal buckets on the sidewalk in front of the shop.

"31b, yeah?" Jermaine asks, walking toward a blue door located just beside the flowers. A large brass knocker shaped like a lion's head stares out at us from the middle of the door.

I nod, reaching into my pocket and taking out the piece of paper I'd torn out of Mom's agenda. I double-check the address again: *31b White Horse Road*. This is definitely it. I carefully fold the paper up and place it back in my pocket. This address is one of the last things Mom wrote before she disappeared.

"I have a bad feeling about this," I say, though Jermaine's finger is already pressing down on the entrance button as the words escape my lips.

After a few moments, a voice crackles through the small speaker above the buzzer.

"Yes?" It's the voice of a little kid. Jermaine and I look at each other.

"Is your Mummy in?" he asks.

A buzzing sound comes from within and the

door clicks to unlock. I pull on the handle and we step inside. The front hall is dim and heavily carpeted. A huge bouquet of flowers sits in a silver vase on top of a small, dark table against the wall.

*"Angel, qien es?"* a woman's voice asks from the top of the stairs.

"Some people to see you, Mummy."

"Haven't I told you never to just let someone in?" The mother's voice is suddenly sharp and angry. I look over at Jermaine. The bad feeling is threatening to suffocate me. He doesn't take his eyes off the landing above us.

A woman appears at the top of the stairs a few seconds later. She's tall and curvaceous and, though it's hard to make out the features of her face in the dim light, my gut tells me she's quite beautiful. I wonder if Jermaine is noticing as well.

"Why, you're only children," she says, the anger dissolving from her voice. "Can I help you? Come up, please." She waves for us to come up the stairs.

Jermaine starts up before me. I follow closely behind, trying to force back my feelings of foreboding. This woman might hold the key to finding Mom: so why am I feeling like I want to turn and run as far away from here as I can get?

Just as I expected, she's really beautiful, with sky-high cheekbones and large, dark eyes that examine us closely as we reach the landing of the stairs. Her eyes scan Jermaine and the welcoming smile disappears briefly.

"Come and sit," she says, motioning us toward

a blood-red velvet sofa. "Are you selling something for your school?"

"Not exactly." I reply, sitting down on the edge of the sofa. Jermaine is quieter now and seems to expect me to take the lead. We sit side-by-side with Cristina in a chair across from us.

"What are you here for then?"

"We're actually here because my mother works for you," I say, hesitating for a just a second. It's difficult to know how much to reveal. My eyes drift downward to my hands, which are folded limply in my lap like a couple of dead, albino fish.

Cristina sits back and regards me silently for a moment. "Really?" she asks flatly. "And just who might your mother be and why do you need to see me?"

"Um, her name is Sydney Fraser. She's Canadian. Well, she does have a bit of an English accent." I'm rambling now. "And she only began working for you a couple of days ago."

Cristina nods, her face relaxing into a smile. "Sydney! Of course I know her. Not like my other girls. Very well-educated." She pauses. "Is she not well? I only ask as she hasn't shown up for the past two days."

"She's fine," Jermaine interrupts.

Cristina turns toward him. "And you are?"

"A family friend. A *close* family friend."

"Very well," she replies dismissively. She turns back and stares hard at me. I feel like an insect under a microscope. "You do look so much like Sydney.

It's odd. She never told me she had any children here with her in London."

Jermaine tenses beside me. I know what he's thinking. It doesn't seem like just an innocent observation. The uneasy feeling I had when we first entered the flat is suddenly back. I need to word my questions about Mom carefully.

"I was just wondering where my Mom's last shift was," I say. I try frantically to think of something to say that would make it seem logical that I'm here, asking her this question, rather than just asking Mom.

"Why?"

Good question. Now I have a few seconds to come up with a halfway decent answer that doesn't make me sound insane.

"Mom left her reading glasses there. I guess she's embarrassed about being sick in bed and all ... when she can't even read the paper."

Cristina stares hard at me again and then her gaze wanders. Something behind me has caught her eye. I turn and see a slim, young boy leaning against the doorframe for the kitchen.

"How impolite of me!" she says. "Would either of you like something to drink? Maybe an orange squash or a fizzy drink?"

I shake my head.

"So your mother has been ill, love," Cristina says, waving her son away with her hand as if he is nothing more than an annoying insect. "Why did she not call in sick? Does she not want her job any longer? I would think it's nearly impossible for a woman in her position to find other employment."

Dizziness sweeps over me like a tsunami. Mom must've said something to her about our situation. What does she know? Or is she just saying it to see how I'll respond?

"She told you why we're in London?" I stammer. Jermaine shoots me a quick glance.

Cristina leans forward, resting her chin on her hands. She smiles at me, with the kind of look people give stray puppies. I don't want her sympathy and feel myself tensing up.

"Yes, Edie, she did. I insist on knowing the women I'm hiring, especially when they ask to be paid under the table."

"My mom didn't return home from work after her first shift," I say. "Do you know where she was cleaning that night? I need to know." My heart is beating so rapidly it feels like it's going to leap out of my chest.

Cristina's eyes darken with concern. "She didn't arrive home? That's not good, is it? I know she finished her job that night without incident because she signed out after her shift that morning."

"But she didn't make it home after that," I say. "Would anyone else have seen her leave? Other cleaners, maybe?"

Cristina nods. "Sylvia, a long-term employee of mine, was on shift with her at the Camden film office." She stands up. "Excuse me for a moment. I need to see what Angel is up to. Boys can get into such mischief, you know." She glances at Jermaine as she speaks.

"Actually, I'll take that orange squash after all. Please," he says.

"Of course. I'll be just a minute. Please, make yourselves at home."

As soon as Cristina is out of sight, Jermaine grabs me by the fleshy part of my upper arm.

"Ow! What are you doing?" I snap. "Playing lobster?"

"Shhh," Jermaine says, placing a finger to his lips. He leans in closer. "We gotta go. You told her way too much. This lady is already concerned that your mum needed to work under the table 'cos that's illegal. And now she finds out your mum's disappeared and you've turned up at her flat."

"So what?" I say, rubbing my biceps. I'm still angry about my arm and the news I've received from Cristina has only convinced me more that something terrible has happened to Mom.

"So, this woman might already be in it up to her neck for employing illegals like your mum and then if the police find out she knew about you and didn't do the right thing by telling them or social services, she'll get it even worse."

"Mom isn't an illegal immigrant. She's got a British passport."

"Don't be daft, Edie. Who cares about that? That woman is likely on the phone right now," he says. "Let's go!"

Jermaine pulls me up from the sofa and this time

I'm more than happy to follow. If he is even half right in his predictions, we're in trouble. It was stupid of me to have said anything about Mom going missing.

Cristina's son appears in the doorway to the kitchen again. This time he's clutching a glass of orange drink in his small hand.

"Where are you going?" he asks, his voice filling with disappointment. "I made this for your friend." He holds out the glass.

"Sorry, just remembered that we're supposed to be somewhere," I say, over my shoulder. Jermaine is already at the stairs, descending them two at a time.

"Mummy! They're leaving!" Angel cries.

I begin to leap down the stairs, keeping my eyes locked on Jermaine's back, praying my feet don't miss a step. Jermaine has already reached the front door and is fumbling with the latch, his fingers clumsy with panic.

I hear commotion above us. Angel's cries of dismay mix with his mother's angry voice. Blood pounds in my ears.

Suddenly the latch clicks and Jermaine twists the door open with his left hand while grabbing my wrist with his right.

"Wait right there!" Cristina shouts from behind me. I can't tell if she's already on the stairs.

Jermaine pulls me through the door then slams it shut with a single, backward kick. We immediately break into a frantic run, our trainer-clad feet slapping up and down on the sidewalk.

A curtain of misty rain wraps itself around us as we continue running without saying a word for what seems like forever. My chest burns and I feel faint, but continue following Jermaine. We reach the high street and continue our mad dash: weaving in and around hand-holding couples, mothers pushing their newborns in strollers, and red-faced joggers. Jermaine leads us back past the Docklands station and down toward the water where we finally slow our pace.

"Just to be safe, let's hang here for a few minutes," Jermaine says, making his way down a set of stone steps to the locks. Below the locks, the murky waters of the Thames wind their way toward the heart of London.

The rain begins to fall harder, making the steps more slippery and treacherous than I would like. A sign posted on the black, wrought-iron rails warns pedestrians about the dangers of walking along the water's edge. That makes me slow down even more.

"You okay?" Jermaine asks from the bottom of the stairs.

"I'm just being careful," I retort. "It's not exactly the safest thing in the world that we're doing, you know." Hopefully he can't tell I'm completely terrified.

Jermaine shrugs his shoulders and watches me continue my snail-like descent, a small, amused smile tugging at the corners of his lips.

I join him a few seconds later, both of us leaning against the railings, me still breathing heavily from both the run and the sheer terror of navigating the stairs.

I look down the river at the boats scurrying along and the tall wharf buildings that dot the waterfront and suddenly feel so tiny and insignificant standing there. A wave of sadness mixed with anger sweeps over me and I back away, tears threatening to race down my cheeks.

"What's up?"

I shake my head. I can't speak. It feels as though someone has sucked my voice away. If I open my mouth, tears will follow. And tears are the last thing I need at this time.

"Hey, don't worry. There's no way that lady will be able to find us, even if she decides to try."

"It's not that," I say. My voice cracks and I pause for a moment. "It's just ... I'm positive something terrible has happened to Mom."

And that's when Jermaine puts his arm around me. That's right — his arm goes around my shoulders and for a split second I forget about everything else except the electrical feeling I'm getting from our bodies touching.

"Naw, couldn't be. If something really bad happened to her, we'd be seeing it on the front of the papers and on the telly and everything."

I appreciate his attempt to make me feel better, but every time I shut my eyes, all I see is my dad's angry face the night we left and all I remember is the feeling of his fingers wrapped around my arm like a boa constrictor.

"C'mon. We're going to find her. You'll see." The concern in Jermaine's voice pulls me back to the present, back to the seemingly constant rain of London and the pleasant heaviness of his arm around my shoulder.

I nod. Tears are forming in my eyes, blurring my vision. I wipe at them with the sleeve of my coat, feeling like a little kid.

"Sorry," I say. "I guess the worry is getting to me. I haven't been able to sleep well since she's been gone." My nose is running and I'm in need of a tissue badly. Mortifying. Now he's going to see me with a drippy, snotty nose: definitely not my most attractive moment.

"Look. We got decent information back there," Jermaine says. "That bird said your mum was up in Camden, right? So that's where we go with the photograph."

"Okay."

Jermaine looks at his watch. "It's not even eleven. I'm starved. Why don't we grab something to eat and then go to Camden?"

I discreetly wipe my nose with the back of my hand.

"Sounds brilliant," I say, trying my London speak for the first time. I feel stronger all of a sudden; I know what I need to do.

## CHAPTER 18

By the time we emerge from Cutty Sark Station, the rain has stopped and the sun is desperately trying to push its way through the grey meringue of clouds. The sun coming out might be a sign that something positive is going to happen. At least that's what I tell myself.

There's a Subway restaurant directly across from the tube station, a reminder of life back in Canada. My stomach aches with longing.

"Hungry?" Jermaine asks.

"Famished," I reply. And, for the first time in a while, I really do have an appetite.

Once inside, we practically throw ourselves at the spotty girl standing behind the counter as the smell of roasted meat and baked bread overwhelms us.

"All right?" she asks, her voice thick with boredom. She twists a lock of ginger hair that is crisp with styling products around her index finger as she watches us scan the plastic menu boards above her head.

"Roast chicken sub on white with pickles, tomato, and mayo," I say. "Loads of pickles. And a coffee," I add, glancing sideways at Jermaine, who is still trying to decide.

"Meatball with loads of hot peppers and pickles," he says. "And extra cheese if you have it."

"Drink?" the girl with the ginger hair asks. She blows a pink gum bubble toward us, then crushes it between her thickly glossed lips with a loud pop.

"A full-fat Coke, yeah?" Jermaine answers. He turns to me and smiles playfully. "Coffee? You going to get all hyper on me?"

My face flushes warmly. "I'm just a bit cold. That's all."

Great. He jokes with me and my response is as wooden as Pinocchio. I wish I could think of something funny or interesting to say. Instead, I stare at my shoes, mortified.

"Ready?" the girl asks. She snaps her gum and holds out her hand. Another bored-looking employee finishes making our sandwiches.

I reach into my knapsack, unzip the inside pocket, and feel around for some of the charity money.

"How much?"

"Eight-pound thirty," she answers, blowing another bubble in my direction.

I hand her the money reluctantly. It's going to run out at some point and that reality is beginning to hit me.

"It's kind of nice to be getting Subway," I say.

"There's so many unfamiliar things here. My best friend, Rume, and I used to get it at lunch whenever we had extra money."

"You have a computer and Internet at your flat?" Jermaine asks as he takes the tray from the girl.

I shake my head. "Are you kidding? We don't even have a home phone yet."

"Well, there's an Internet café upstairs here," he says, and, as though reading my mind, is already heading toward the stairs.

The café turns out to be no more than ten or twelve computers that are dinosaur-age old. They're separated from the main part of the restaurant by a cheap-looking plastic partition.

We sit down at one of the tables and Jermaine unwraps his sub. Even though I'm starving, I find it hard to think about eating.

Glancing at my watch, I do a quick mental calculation of the time difference between London and Toronto. It's about ten to seven in the morning in Toronto. Rume always gets up early. She likes to check to see if she's had overnight emails from her cousins in Bangladesh. I smile. It might just work; I might catch her on MSN.

Butterflies of excitement tickle my stomach as I log into my Hotmail account.

"Your password is Peaches2000?" Jermaine laughs through a mouthful of meatballs, bread, and tomato sauce.

"Yeah, it is. Do you have a problem with it?" I ask, half-jokingly. The thought of what might have become of Peaches still causes an instant lump in my throat.

"It just sounds like a stripper's name or something."

I turn away from the computer and raise an eyebrow at him. "Takes one to know one," I said.

Clearly, I'm a complete failure in the witty, flirty comeback department.

Jermaine stares at me. "Sometimes you're kind of strange, Edie," he says.

"Yeah, I was aware of that. Thanks," I hope some massive, science fiction–inspired rift opens up and takes me away to another dimension. Why am I such an awkward nerd around guys? Rume understood me. We understood each other. I turn back to the computer screen.

*R u there? It's me, Edie.*

I wait, my fingers hovering over the grey plastic squares of the computer keyboard in anticipation.

And, suddenly, there it is, appearing on the screen like a mirage: a response from Rume.

*Oh my god! Is it really u? Where have u gone? I miss u so much, girl!*

*London. In England, not Ontario. Long story. I miss u too!*

I glance over at Jermaine. Though he's pretending to be absorbed in eating his sandwich, it's obvious he's trying to read the computer screen whenever he thinks I'm not paying attention. As soon as he sees me looking, he quickly diverts his attention toward a couple arguing at a nearby table.

*When r u coming back? I have Peaches. Found her sitting on your front steps looking hungry. I guess she was waiting for you to come back too. She misses you.*

"Oh my god!" I say, grabbing Jermaine excitedly, which nearly results in a meatball and tomato disaster happening on his lap.

"Blimey! I'd rather eat it than wear it, Edie."

"Sorry, sorry!" I say, breathlessly. "My cat. Peaches. That's why I have the username. My best friend has her!"

Jermaine laughs. "Your cat created your username?"

I punch him playfully on the arm. "No, dummy! My cat's name is Peaches. We couldn't bring her when we came here and didn't have time to find her a new home." I pause for a moment, remembering the last time I saw Peaches curled up on my bed. "But she's safe. She's with my best friend, Rume."

"That's brilliant," Jermaine says. "Why didn't you find her a new home, though?"

"Long story," I say, turning back to the screen. Not even Rume knows everything about Mom and I. "I'll log off soon and we can go."

Thankfully, Jermaine doesn't push for any more information, and, instead, goes back to devouring his sandwich.

*I'll write soon and tell u more. Give Peaches loads of kisses for me.*

I exit my email and grab my sandwich.

"Let's get out of here," I say.

"What about eating?" Jermaine asks.

"Not important," I say. "We need to find my mom."

We stand up and make our way to the first floor of the restaurant. Outside, London waits. And somewhere in the city is the answer to Mom's disappearance.

# CHAPTER 19

Throngs of people fill the sidewalk outside the Camden Town tube station. The atmosphere reminds me of a circus. Like Toronto, the people are diverse: someone from every part of the globe seems to walk by in the few seconds I spend standing still on the sidewalk. A middle-aged Rasta man in a vibrant knit hat casually lights a joint while a young American couple talks loudly about the evils of drug use as they stroll by, cameras slung around their necks. And the air is heavy with smells: dried spices mingle with the odour of fried onions and meat from the street vendors, the sweet smokiness of marijuana mixes with the sweaty scent of thousands of bodies, and, as always, the smell of London itself, is there, underneath it all, a mixture of ancient damp and exhaust fumes.

"We need to head in this direction," Jermaine says, crooking his thumb to the right. "The street vendors will probably know where this place is and they may even have seen something. I bet loads of them set up really early. I reckon they're the eyes and ears of this place."

"Do you really think they'd have been around when Mom was getting off work?"

Jermaine shrugs. "Dunno, really. Thing is, if she was around for a bit that morning, they're likely the ones who'd have seen her."

Within the first few minutes of walking, we pass at least a dozen booths set up to lure tourists into buying cheaply made replica soccer jerseys with Rooney's and Beckham's names printed across the back. Everything is so flashy and funky. I wish I had money to shop. I imagine walking down the street with deep red streaks in my hair, wearing a short denim skirt and a pair of platform boots like the ones on display in the shop windows here. I'd be reinvented: a new Edie for a new city, finally leaving my painful history in Canada behind. Except a new start would mean nothing without Mom.

"Where exactly are we going?" I ask.

"Not sure. I've never been here before," Jermaine replies.

I stop. "What do you mean you've never been here? How are we supposed to have a chance of finding my mom?"

"I've spent most of my life in South London. Why would I go all over London? The only time I'm north of the river is usually for school trips and stuff. Me and my brother used to think we were on holiday when we'd go to Electric Avenue in Brixton to the shops with our mum."

I open my mouth to apologize, though I'm not exactly sure what for. But before I can say anything, Jermaine veers off to the right and down a wide alley where several different sorts of vendors are set up.

I follow him as he saunters toward a doughnut stand. The sign at the top of the both is adorned with an American flag, and, in red-and-gold lettering, the words DELICIOUS AMERICAN DOUGHNUTS.

"Show him the photo," Jermaine says.

The man working the doughnut stand looks a little like one of the deep-fried pastries he's selling. He's nearly as wide as he is high and his eyes glitter like two jewels from within his bloated face.

I pull the photograph of Mom out of my coat pocket, my fingers treating it as gently as a glass egg. I don't want to look at it. I can't.

"Can I help you, Miss?" the doughnut man asks. His eyes are kind.

I nod. The lump in my throat is back.

A large, burly man wearing an Arsenal soccer jersey and smelling strongly of beer combined with wet dog steps in front of me.

"'Ello, mate. Two of them chocolate ones with the hundreds of thousands on top," he growls, rummaging around in the front pocket of his jeans for money.

Jermaine rolls his eyes at me and kisses his teeth loudly at the man who is now handing over a five-pound note while simultaneously stuffing one of the doughnuts into his mouth. Renegade sprinkles cling to his bottom lip. As soon as he moves out of the way, I take a deep breath and step forward.

"I'm hoping you can help me, actually," I say. "We're looking for this woman. She's … a relative. Last seen around here."

The man looks hard at me and then at the photograph of Mom. He shakes his head.

"Sorry, love. Haven't seen her. And I certainly would've remembered a lady that beautiful if she'd come this way," he says. "Is it drugs?"

"What?" I ask.

"Drugs. Is that why she's on the street?" he shakes his head. "They claim too many in this city. The need for the needle turns them into zombies, doesn't it?"

I begin to shake. "No. She is not on drugs. That's not it at all," I snap.

"I didn't mean to offend you, Miss. None of my business," he says apologetically.

"No it's not," I say. "But thanks, anyway." I put the photo back in my pocket. Finding Mom is going to be impossible.

"Can I at least offer you a free doughnut?" he asks, waving a shovel-sized hand over the colourful display of pastries.

"No, thanks." A sharp jab to my ribs causes me turn around. I glare at Jermaine.

"You best get a doughnut," he says, nodding enthusiastically toward a row of Boston creams. "You've hardly eaten anything today." He looks at the man. "My sister. What can I say? She gets so focused on things that she forgets to take care of herself."

"Your sister? She's your sister?" the man asks.

"Looks more like our father," Jermaine replies.

"Actually, a Boston cream would be great. Thank you," I interject, wanting to get out of there.

The man carefully extracts one of the doughnuts from the row, its shiny, brown icing cracking under the pressure of the metal tongs. He places it on a piece of waxed paper and hands it to me.

"Good luck on your search," he says. "I'm sure she's looking forward to seeing you as well."

I nod and quickly walk away, tears welling up in my eyes once more. Mom will be trying to get back to me as well … if she's able to.

"Wait up," Jermaine says, falling into stride beside me. He touches my elbow. "It will all work out, Edie."

I turn around and practically shove the doughnut at him. "How do you know it will be okay? You still have your mom. That makes it really easy for you to say everything will work out, doesn't it? You're not going to be an orphan at the end of the day!"

Jermaine holds up his hands, palms forward, in the universal sign of surrender.

"Wait a minute," he says. "I'm the one helping you here. Remember? And, like I said before, my mum is really sick. The stress of my brother's death and the mess that followed really affected her. She's in pain a lot of the time. And it kills me seeing her like that. You're not the only one who has it tough, Edie."

The anger drains from me, leaving me feeling deflated, like a forgotten birthday-party balloon. He's right. For the last few years, I've been so wrapped up in what Mom and I are constantly going through, that I hardly notice other people's issues.

"Why is she in pain?"

Jermaine puts his head in his hands for a moment.

"She has Sickle Cell. Stress makes it really bad."

"And your brother?" I ask. The doughnut begins to shake in my hand as soon as the words are out of my mouth. Do I really want to know the answer to this?

Jermaine raises an eyebrow at me. "I can tell you heard. Who filled you in on the urban myth? Was it Keisha? Man, that cow has a big mouth. She just be hoping no one remembers her mother walking around drunk in Tesco nude two years ago, thinking there was a special naturalist night on."

"Her mom really did that?" I ask, incredulous.

"Yeah." He smiles. "Can you imagine her shopping list? Milk, rice, and, most important of all, knickers!"

I nod. "God, I was horrible to you just now. I'm really, really sorry. I just don't know how we'll ever find my mom here. There's too many people and the city is so huge."

"We need to take a walk and clear our heads." Jermaine says. "I think that the canal is around here."

# CHAPTER 20

"The thing is, Edie, no one really cares what happened to my brother. Not really. What people care about is the drama of it all. It's the community's own little reality TV show."

I nod. We're walking along the canal's edge and the view is stunning. There are cyclists humming along, people having leisurely drinks at waterside patios, and loads of brightly painted houseboats bobbing peacefully at their moorings like corks in the water.

"I didn't kill my brother or our friends," Jermaine says. "However, I'm the only one still alive from that day and I guess my word doesn't mean much."

"How old were you when it happened?" I ask.

"I was eight. My brother, Jerome, was ten. So were most of our friends. That's why they let me be the superhero that day."

"What do you mean, they 'let you be the superhero'?"

Jermaine laughs. "I was always bothering Jerome, tagging along. And he was so good about it. He was always so good about it. It was Saturday, you know? He should've just wanted to hang with his friends, but he let me come along."

We're passing one of the houseboats. A young couple sits on the deck, drinking wine and laughing. The woman has the shiniest red hair I've ever seen and is wearing a floral dress that looks expensive. It makes me jealous to see people that seem so carefree, especially adults. They're the ones who are supposed to have big problems and worries, not kids like Jermaine and me.

"And that day there was this abandoned BMW in the car park of our estate. It had been there for weeks. We decided we'd play Superhero. One of us would rescue everyone else from the car. We'd pretend there was an accident and the superhero would save everyone from the ... the burning car."

Jermaine pauses and already the terribleness of what he's about to tell me is sinking in.

"The plan was that Billy would light these matches he nicked from his father and then I'd rescue them. Only the doors locked somehow and I couldn't open them and ..."

We stop walking. Jermaine leans his arms against the railings and looks out over the water.

"They died in the car?" I ask. "In the fire?"

He nods and drops his head onto his forearms.

"But that's not your fault. Anyone with half a brain should've figured out it was an accident." I'm not sure whom, Jermaine or myself, I'm trying to convince by stating the obvious.

He lifts his head and looks straight at me. His dark eyes are heavy with sadness. "Yeah, the police and everyone eventually believed me, but Billy's dad kicked in my mum's door that night and threatened to kill me, which she didn't really need, considering her oldest son had just died." He laughs, a bitter laugh that seems to come from far away. "It's funny how I became the villain in the story, innit? But maybe that's 'cos Billy's dad is white and I'm black. There are loads of people in the community who have decided to mark me for life."

"Including teachers at school," I say.

"Including loads of people at school," he says.

We stop talking for a few minutes. I've wanted to tell someone my secret for so long. The secret Mom and I hide each time we move. Jermaine is the only person that knows Mom is gone. Now I want to tell him the whole truth.

"Mom and I haven't really spoken about the night we left my father since it happened," I say. It's hard for me to believe I'm actually going to confide in someone about what happened the night our life was turned upside down. Even Rume doesn't have a clue that Mom and I were on the run when we moved to Regent Park. And she still doesn't know we're on the run, though she might be wondering after my email.

"When I was a little girl, my life looked perfect from the outside. My dad is a psychologist for the police and we had a really nice house with two cars and a big yard. We went on nice vacations. I've even been to Disney World in Florida twice. No one knew the truth of what was happening in our house, though. I was always good in school, so none of the teachers suspected a thing."

"Teachers also don't care enough to notice or to ask if they do suspect stuff," Jermaine says.

"My teachers were great," I say. "They cared about us, but I guess they didn't think bad stuff happened in nice areas like the one I used to live in."

I pause. Am I ready to unleash my memories? I fear it might be a bit like opening Pandora's Box. Jermaine continues watching me. I appreciate his silence.

"The thing was, my dad has a bad temper. Really bad. It was hard to tell what would cause my dad to get angry. Sometimes it was as simple as a glass being dropped on the floor or a bad day at work. But he always hit Mom and never me … until the night we left."

I remember everything so clearly; I was working on a school project, sitting on the floor of our den. At dinner, my father drank three glasses of Scotch and was very quiet. This was usually a sign that things weren't good and that Mom and I should be as invisible as possible. But I wanted to do well on that project. I loved my grade four teacher, Ms. Sherman. She always made me feel like I could achieve anything and I wanted to make her proud.

That's why I didn't put away my papers and markers and scissors when my father sat down in his leather chair with the remainder of the bottle of Scotch to watch the hockey game.

"What happened that night?" Jermaine asks.

"I refused to clean up a school project I was working on and go to bed early."

Images from the past are coming back, tumbling freely into my mind. It's like I've pressed Play on the DVD of my life.

I'd glanced over at the television after defying my father. A player in a blue-and-white hockey jersey had just violently thrust his elbow into an opposing player's face. A whistle blew.

"Go to bed, Edie. And clean … that … mess … up. *Now.*"

I remember taking a deep breath. I wanted the project to be good. And I remember being tired of walking on eggshells around my father when he was like this.

"No. I don't want to," I whispered.

Suddenly, I was back with Jermaine. Back in London, beside Regent's Canal with the sun just beginning to shine and warm my back as we leaned over the railings. I didn't want to remember.

"You okay?" Jermaine asks. "Don't tell me if it's too hard."

I shake my head; it's too late. And I want to get this out, to have someone know what's happened to me. "He moved so fast, like a cheetah. One minute I was sitting cross-legged on our blue shag rug. The next minute I was in the air and sailing toward the wall."

"Damn," Jermaine says, his voice barely more than a whisper.

"All I really remember after that is my mother screaming about needing to take me to the hospital, then my dad making stupid, drunken apologies while putting me to bed with an ice pack on my shoulder. Later that night, Mom woke me up and told me to be quiet because we were leaving. We ended up in a shelter for women and children for a few weeks, but once we moved out and into our own place, he kept finding us."

"What would he do when he found you?" Jermaine asks.

"He'd phone and either beg Mom to come back or threaten her. He always thought she was dating other men. Like she had time for that. And he'd park outside our house for hours, sometimes overnight. Crazy stuff. So we'd pick up and run again. We even moved to Vancouver to try and escape him. But it didn't work. That's why we're here now."

"And you think your dad has something to do with all of this? With your mum disappearing?"

"I'll bet my life he has something to do with it," I reply. "It's like I can feel his presence in my bones. He's been trying to track us down nonstop since that night. He'll stop at nothing to get his family back." I turn and look directly at Jermaine. "What I'm really afraid of is that if something has happened to Mom," my voice wavers, "that I'll be sent back to him. I'd rather be put in Children's Aid."

Jermaine nods. He doesn't have to say anything; I know he understands.

We both gaze out at the couple on the houseboat. The guy is now reading a newspaper and the woman is setting down a platter of what looks like fruit and cheese. Their wineglasses have been refilled. I wonder how many rich people in London know or even care that millions of us in the city are leading lives so completely different than their own.

# CHAPTER 21

The concierge sitting behind the desk at the Camden film office is a small man with sharp, elf-like features. In fact, he's so small, if it wasn't for the bald spot at the crown of his head, I might've mistaken him for a kid.

"Can I help you?" he asks haughtily after we stand in front of the desk for a few moments, waiting for him to acknowledge we exist. The final Harry Potter book sits open in front of him. He's holding his page with his left index finger. It's clear we're interrupting his reading and that he's less than impressed.

"Hopefully," I say, removing the photograph of Mom from my pocket once again. "Do you recognize this woman?"

"Should I?" he asks, arching an eyebrow at me. He begins to drum the fingers of his right hand against the desktop, slowly and deliberately.

"Um, she sometimes cleans here. At night."

At that point, I swear he rolls his eyes. Gritting my teeth, I continue to smile even though I want to punch him in his arrogant face. He closes his book, takes the photo and quickly looks at it. My heart beats rapidly in anticipation.

"I'm only here during the day," he says, his words clipped. "So, I'm afraid I can't help you. Anything else?" he asks as he hands the photo back. Then, without waiting for my answer, he reopens his book and begins reading again. Clearly he's finished with us.

"Excuse me, mate," Jermaine says, placing his hands palm down on the desk and leaning forward. "But it's really important that we find this lady."

This time there's no mistaking the frostiness in the concierge's gaze. He places his index finger back in the book and fixes his eyes on Jermaine.

"May I ask why you two are looking for this woman and not someone more ..." he pauses and looks Jermaine up and down. "More official?"

My heart sinks. This is the only place I really felt might give us a solid lead for finding Mom. Now it appears to be to be a complete dead-end.

"Isn't there anyone here that might be able to help us?" I ask. "The woman in the photo is my mom and I have good reason to believe she's in danger."

Jermaine glances at me, a look of surprise sweeping across his face. I don't care if this pompous midget of a man knows that I'm desperate. I'm tired of keeping what Mom and I have to go through a secret. It isn't fair. We didn't do anything to deserve a life where we need to constantly run like criminals.

The concierge pauses for a moment, letting his

irritation at being disrupted settle like toxic dust. He looks at me and sighs.

"I suppose Thomas might be of help," he says reluctantly. After paging Thomas on the phone, he goes back to reading his book without another word.

We sit down on a green plastic couch to wait for Thomas. Neither of us says anything.

After what seems like forever, the steel doors of the elevators slide open and a tall, bald man with a neck like a steel beam steps out.

He walks over to us. "Can I help you two?" he asks. His voice is surprisingly gentle and soft for a man of his size.

I nod and show him the photograph.

"We're looking for my mom," I say. "She was cleaning here a couple of nights ago."

Thomas looks at the photo, runs a hand along the smooth skin of his brown scalp, and laughs. "Of course I remember her! Loved her accent. Gorgeous woman, she is."

My heart begins to hammer with anticipation. I quickly put the photo back in my pocket so that Thomas and Jermaine won't notice my hands shaking.

"Did you happen to see her leave the building that morning? Like after she was done her shift?"

"Sure. I'm usually just coming on duty then. We need to let the cleaners out because the building still locked up at that time."

Hope surges through my body. "Did my mom say where she was going when she left?"

"Funny that. She did, actually. I guess she didn't know the buses well because she asked me where the nearest place to get a good cup of coffee was and which bus would get her back to New Cross or Lewisham the quickest. I told her there was a Starbucks that would be open right by the 29 stop and that the 29 would take her to Trafalgar Square where she could pretty much catch a bus to wherever she needed in South London."

"So last you saw her, she was headed for Trafalgar Square, then?" Jermaine asks.

Thomas slowly nods. "Well, last I saw her, she was headed out that door," he says, pointing to the glass doors at the entrance of the building, "on and her way to Starbucks."

We hastily thank Thomas and hurry back outside before he can ask any questions. Jermaine whistles loudly at the concierge and gives him a sarcastic wave goodbye on our way out. The concierge shoots him a withering death stare in return.

"I guess we retrace Mom's steps," I say, breathing deeply. I feel alive and optimistic. By the end of the day, I'm going to be with Mom. I just know I am.

# CHAPTER 22

I order a coffee from the barista at Starbucks and then show her the photo of Mom. She shakes her head.

"I wasn't working that day," she says, handing me a steaming paper cup of coffee. "But I think Simon was on. Just a minute and I'll get him for you."

Simon finishes putting whipped cream on top of a drink and comes over. He's really young and really cute with spiky blond hair and blue eyes that dance when he smiles.

"Hiya," he says.

"Hi," I say, smiling widely back at him. I recognize the accent from the old Crocodile Dundee movies Mom used to watch when I was little. He's Australian — and gorgeous. I continue smiling.

"Edie," Jermaine hisses, giving me a slight shove.

"Um, yeah. So the girl that served us said you were working the other day. This is a long-shot, but we think my mom came in here and I was hoping you might recognize her." I put the photograph on the counter.

Simon peers at it. "Is she your birth mother or something? Are you adopted?"

"What?" I ask, confused.

"Are you looking for your biological mother? Is this her?"

"Sort of," I reply. "I mean, yeah that's her."

"I remember her. She came in with a man. Her boyfriend or something?"

All the blood in my body rushes to my feet. I nod at Simon, though I'm not sure if I really want to hear anything else.

"They were arguing something fierce. That's why I remember them."

I can feel hot tears welling in my eyes. Everything blurs.

"What did he look like? The guy she was with?" I ask, my voice cracking.

"I shouldn't have said anything," Simon says apologetically.

I shake my head. "I'm okay," I say, taking a deep breath. I need to be stronger than this.

"Decent-looking bloke, probably about fifty. Black hair. Dark eyes."

That's all I need to hear. I grab Jermaine by the arm. "We need to go. Now," I say.

He nods. "Thanks so much,' he says to Simon.

"Hey, your coffee!" I hear Simon shout as we run out the door.

"Why do you carry around his work number if

he's such a wanker?" Jermaine asks. He watches me leaf through my diary, the same one that, only a few days ago, was unceremoniously kicked around on the wet ground by Precious and her cronies.

"I don't know … he's my dad."

"But he's a complete twat. No offense."

I stop looking through the diary for a moment. "I guess I always hoped that somehow things would change."

"You mean like a fairytale ending? One day you ring your dad and suddenly he becomes Mr. Nice Guy?" Jermaine asks, leaning back against the bench we're sitting on and lacing his hands behind his head.

"I'm not stupid, if that's what you mean," I snap. I go back to searching for Dad's number.

"No, I don't mean that. It's just I don't even know who my father is," Jermaine says. "Sometimes I see someone on the train or just walking down the high street and catch a glimpse of myself in the bloke's eyes or in the shape of his lips and I wonder. But I don't really give a toss. I don't need him."

I put my finger on the page where I scrawled Dad's work number in blue ink a couple of years ago.

"Can you hand me that phone card?" I ask.

Jermaine reaches into his pocket. "You okay to do this? What if they put him on the phone?"

I smile at Jermaine. "That would be a dream come true at this point."

I tear the plastic off the phone card and flip open Jermaine's mobile phone.

As the phone begins to ring far away on the other side of the Atlantic Ocean, I glance at my watch. It's two o'clock. That means it's nine in the morning in Toronto. Dad will have been at work for at least an hour already. He likes to be in his office early.

The phone stops ringing and the click of the receiver being picked up sounds in my ear. There's a brief moment of silence.

"Toronto Police Services. How may we help you?"

I'm not sure if I can speak. Words stick in my throat like peanut butter.

"May I speak with Bryce Fraser?" I finally manage to choke out.

"One moment, please." I'm put on hold.

Jermaine looks at me questioningly. 'What's up?' he mouths.

"On hold," I say, flashing him a thumbs-up.

"Hello? I'm sorry, but Doctor Fraser is out of the office for two weeks. May I take a message?"

My hand begins to shake. "Did he leave a contact number?"

Out of the corner of my eye, I notice Jermaine's expression darken with concern.

"We wouldn't be able to give out that kind of information even if he did, Miss."

I pause. It's useless to even ask whether he's away on holiday or if they know his whereabouts. The answer will be the same. And there's no way I'm going to risk identifying myself just to get answers.

"Well, thanks anyway," I say.

"What happened? You're as white as a ghost," Jermaine says as I finish the call.

"He didn't say anything. He's out of the office for two weeks. This is exactly what I was afraid of. Seriously, it's like he has some sort of evil magical power and can pick up our scent, no matter how hard we try to escape." I hand his phone back and bury my head in my hands.

Mom needs me. I know this. We've been in danger all along; that's why she moved us here: for one last chance at having a normal life.

I sit up, tuck my diary securely back into my bag, and look at Jermaine.

"Let's go," I say, standing up.

"Go where?" Jermaine asks. "You really think your dad is here in London? There are loads of places he could've gone on holiday."

"I know my dad. We need to just keep retracing Mom's steps the morning she disappeared and see if we can find any further clues about what happened to her."

"And what if there aren't any clues?" Jermaine asks, falling into step with me as I hurry to the bus stop.

I look at him, my lips pressed into a tight grimace. "That's not an option. I have to find her."

## CHAPTER 23

"Ouch!" I cry out as the bus lurches sharply to the right, sending me to the left, causing my elbow to connect hard with a metal railing. Navigating the stairs of the bus is more difficult than I expected. I mean, I know I'm a klutz at the best of times, but come on! It's like trying to dance on the deck of a ship in the middle of a stormy sea.

Jermaine keeps laughing even after we reach two seats at the front of the upper deck of the bus and sit down. "Haven't you ever been at the top of a bus before?" he asks.

I rub my elbow. "We don't have stupid, two-storey buses in Toronto. At least not ones for regular people; they're only for tourists."

"Blimey," Jermaine says, still laughing. "You'll get your legs for it soon enough. And since you're still a bit of a tourist, you'll get the best view of London from here."

The view from the top floor of the bus is pretty amazing. The streets of London stretch out in front of us, bustling with people and activity. Leaning forward, I rest my arms on railing and my chin on my hands. I think about what Jermaine said about the likelihood of Dad actually being in London. I desperately want to believe he's right; that the probability of Dad coming here of all the places in the world is next to nothing. But I can't shake the feeling in the pit of my stomach. When it comes to controlling and destroying my life and Mom's, if the past is anything to go by, the probability that he's here is actually very, very good.

As the bus pulls away from the curb once more, fat raindrops begin to splatter onto the windows. The smell of French fries, vinegar, and ketchup fills the air and I instinctively turn to see where the smell is coming from. My stomach rumbles uneasily as two guys around our age walk onto the upper deck with soggy cardboard takeout boxes. One boy, who's built like a tree stump, surveys all the passengers, a smirk plastered across his acne-riddled face.

"Shut yer pie hole, ya bleedin' poof!" the other boy shouts back down the stairs at someone. He's wearing a red Arsenal football jersey and his hair looks like it's taking a vacation from water and shampoo.

They jostle into seats a few rows behind us. I roll my eyes at Jermaine. The smell of the fries is making my stomach do hungry somersaults and that's when I make the mistake of turning around again to glance at the two of them.

The shorter one, with the raised blotches of acne

running along both cheeks and across the width of his forehead, notices me first. Nudging his friend, he stuffs a massive wad of fries into his mouth, smiles grotesquely, and winks at me. It isn't a friendly wink, but more of a suggestive smirk. I feel my face flush hotly in embarrassment and annoyance. I quickly turn back around.

"I think we're getting close to Leicester Square. It's where all the big movie openings are held and all the actors come and walk along the red carpet giving out autographs and stuff. See?" Jermaine moves closer to me and points out the window.

I look out the window to where he's pointing. There are loads of people and restaurants, including the biggest Burger King I've ever seen. But it's pretty hard to concentrate on anything outside the bus for too long with Jermaine so close to me. He reaches over and takes my hand. The feeling of his skin touching mine sends tiny shocks through my body. Every cell in my body is warm and tingly.

And that's when I hear it.

"Oi, beautiful!"

I know it's one of those idiots behind us and am not about to give them the satisfaction of me turning around and showing them that I heard or cared.

But the atmosphere in the bus seems to have changed; the air has thickened with tension like a well-cooked pudding. Several passengers suddenly become more interested in their newspapers and novels.

"Oi, lovely! Come on back here and give us a

cuddle and squeeze, rather than wasting yer time with that jungle monkey."

The woman across from us draws in a sharp breath and Jermaine's hand tenses against mine. I don't believe in God, but find myself pleading with whatever higher power might be up there to make the two idiots spontaneously combust. If this were Toronto, lots of passengers would've said something by now, but no one on this bus is reacting at all, aside from one woman who hurriedly gathers her shopping bags, grabs her daughter's hand, and retreats downstairs. Everyone else continues to ignore the situation like turtles retreating into their shells.

"Let's get off," I whisper to Jermaine. The feeling of dread I've been experiencing on and off since Mom's disappearance is intensifying.

"Yeah, let's. 'Cos that's just what those tossers want, innit?" Jermaine shoots back, his voice thick with sarcasm.

Before I can even reply, something hits the back of my head. It doesn't hurt and the impact is hardly enough to even startle me. I reach back. Whatever it is, it's soggy and warm and stuck in my hair. Gross. I pull it out. A French fry dangles limply between my thumb and index finger, its greasy surface still coated in ketchup.

From behind me, raucous hoots of laughter ring out.

My face is hot with anger. I'm as furious with myself for not saying anything to the idiots as I am with this whole, stupid situation. Our bus rolls past the entrance for the National Portrait Gallery and then we're in Trafalgar Square. I recognize the gun-metal grey lion statues and long, fingerlike column from photos and movies. Masses of tourists are milling around in the square, some taking photographs, others perching on the edge of the fountains or feeding the pigeons.

"Next stop, we're off," Jermaine says, getting out of his seat. He's still holding on to my hand, but now it feels like a gesture of defiance more than anything else.

There's a flash of red and suddenly the boy in the Arsenal jersey is standing in front of us.

"Leaving so soon?" he asks, spittle flying from his bottom lip as he speaks.

"We don't want any trouble," Jermaine begins, but the boy cuts him off.

"Nice one. You lot have brought us nothing but trouble. Maybe you should've thought about not wanting trouble before you left your own country, yeah?"

"I'm British," Jermaine says, a hard edge creeping into his voice. "South London born and bred."

The boy reaches behind his back and pulls something out of his back pocket. All I see is a flash of sliver. It's a knife. I freeze behind Jermaine.

"Like I said, I don't want any trouble," Jermaine repeats. This time his voice is low and even. He grasps my hand tightly as he speaks. The bus lurches away from Trafalgar Square. We've missed our stop. The world suddenly seems to be moving in slow motion.

The boy smirks, drawing his lips back from his yellow teeth like a rabid dog. He looks Jermaine right in the eye.

"Blacks ain't British," he says. "You was brought here to serve us."

The crown of Jermaine's head connects with the boy's chest with an audible, cracking thud. A surprised and enraged roar emits from the boy in response to the attack.

"Look here!" shouts an elderly man in a well-worn brown suit who just neatly folded his newspaper in half in preparation for getting off the bus.

Seconds later, I'm being pulled along the aisle and down the stairs to the lower platform of the bus. I don't dare look back, though several people are yelling down to the driver.

"Don't stop if the driver comes out," Jermaine shouts over his shoulder to me. The panic in his voice sends shivers through my body. "That prat isn't going to care if he kills me right here. And I don't fancy ending up being another Stephen Lawrence."

We land on the lower level of the bus with a thud and dash toward the open back exit. Though the bus isn't moving very quickly, I can't believe it when Jermaine lets go of my hand and leaps out of the bus and onto the sidewalk with the fluidity and grace of a cat.

He looks back at me and waves frantically, signalling to me to jump. I stand, frozen.

"Edie! Jump!" he shouts. The urgency in his

voice propels me into action. I hold my breath as if I'm about to leap from a high diving board and throw myself toward him.

I slam into Jermaine and we fall together onto the pavement in a heap. The bus rounds the corner and continues out of sight.

He helps me up. "You okay?" he asks. Several people stare at us disapprovingly as they pass by.

Embarrassed, I wipe at my jeans. "That was totally terrifying. I thought he was going to kill you back there."

"Yeah. I can't say I'm not relieved myself," he says. "There's no doubt, given the chance, he'd have slit me open like a pig."

"Shouldn't we tell someone? Go to the police or something?"

"Wouldn't do any good, Edie. If I tell them some bloke was after me with a knife on a bus, they'll just think it was some kind of gang thing and that I done something to deserve it." He laughs.

"It's not funny," I say. "How can you not be furious? I mean that guy was a total racist pig."

Jermaine shrugs. "If I got mad every time somebody was racist against me, I'd be fighting every day of my life. I've managed to stay out of gangs this long 'cos I don't want to have one foot in the grave every day. I pick my battles. If I don't, I might end up like Stephen Lawrence or Anthony Walker or one of them lot."

"Who are they?' I ask, as we begin walking back toward Trafalgar Square.

"Some black blokes who got murdered 'cos of their colour," he says matter-of-factly.

We walk along without speaking for a few moments. The more I find out about London, the less I like it. Racially motivated murders, knife-wielding psychopaths on buses ... not to mention people who decided to blow themselves and everyone around them up on the subway.

"I'll tell you what though," Jermaine says.

"What?"

"You make London exciting. Escaping from the lady your mum used to work for and getting attacked by racist wanks with knives. What's next?"

I don't answer. All I can think about was how he just used the past tense when speaking about Mom.

# CHAPTER 24

I'm beginning to realize that finding Mom in a city as massive as London is going to be impossible without some sort of miracle. Going to the police is starting to look like the only choice I have left. The charity money isn't going to last forever and I'll need a place to live, even if that means having Children's Aid involved.

"Hungry?" Jermaine asks.

Despite the craziness of the bus ride and not being any closer to finding Mom, I am feeling hungry.

"Yeah, I could eat. Want to grab some fries or something?"

"I thought we could spend some of that money on a meal that was a bit more posh. Seeing how I'm taking the rap for stealing it and everything."

I think about it. There's still a decent amount of money left, but I already decided if there was any remaining when I found Mom, it should be given back to the school or donated to a charity. It seems wrong to spend it on a dinner for me and Jermaine and at a restaurant. But the idea of having a nice meal with him sends shivers through me.

"Where did you want to go?" I ask.

"Greenwich? Maybe Pizza Express or something like that. I can show you the *Cutty Sark*, like I promised."

I smile. "Sounds amazing," I say, trying not to remember how originally Jermaine promised to show me the *Cutty Sark* after we found Mom.

The restaurant is packed by the time we get to Greenwich. That doesn't matter because it's just nice to be on a date. Moving nearly every year has been disastrous for my love life. I'll start to get to know a guy and maybe have a chance to mess around a few times with him at a party or something and then Mom and I leave again. Because of that, I've never really had a boyfriend.

Jermaine holds open the glass door to the restaurant for me as I step inside. Harried-looking waiters and waitresses rush by us without a passing glance and for a moment I wonder if we'll be ignored until we give up and leave.

Finally, a red-faced waitress stops in front of us. "Table for two?" she asks, straining her voice above the noise coming from several nearby tables with young children. A transparent bead of sweat trickles slowly down her right temple.

I nod. As she leads us to our table, I look around at the polished wooden floors and tiny vases, each holding one red flower, on the tables. This is nicer than any restaurant I've been to since we left Dad. When Mom and I were first on the run, she'd take me to Swiss Chalet for a chicken dinner whenever there was a little money to spare. After a couple of years of running, there never seemed to be any extra money.

The waitress seats us at a table in the corner near the open kitchen where we can watch the pizzas being made. A tiny candle flickers and splutters in the middle of the table as if desperately trying to stay lit.

"I think I need to go to the police," I say as soon as we sit down. I keep my voice low. The table next to us is close enough to reach out and touch.

Jermaine's eyes widen. "Why would you want to do that?'

"I can't go on like this, that's why. Plus, what if my dad is here and is holding Mom hostage or something?"

"There's already been community officers around yours," he says, his face darkening. "You might end up with him or in care. Besides, the police around here don't always help."

A different waitress appears at our table, forcing us to end the conversation. She is very beautiful, with dark hair and full lips the colour of the wine. I feel a twinge of jealousy as she smiles at Jermaine.

"Anything to drink? Coke? Fizzy water?"

"I'll have a Coke, yeah," Jermaine says. "And an American Hot Pizza."

"Me too," I say. "I mean I'll have a Coke. But diet." I quickly scan the menu. The waitress puts a hand on her hip. I can feel her impatience radiating in waves toward me.

"And, um, I'll have the Four Seasons pizza," I say, deciding on the first pizza that is easy to pronounce. I don't want to look like a fool in front of Jermaine.

The waitress nods curtly, scribbles down a few words on her little pad of paper, and sweeps the menus off our table.

Once she's out of earshot, Jermaine leans forward, elbows on the table.

"The police will ring council services straightaway and they'll put you in a care home until they find out what's happening with your mum, you know."

"I know," I say, trying to sound determined.

"They might even deport you. Without your mum, how can you stay? And if your dad is just on holiday, they'll likely ring him and have you sent straight back to Canada to live with him."

I chew nervously on my bottom lip. I hadn't thought of that. If there's no proof Dad is involved in Mom's disappearance, and, let's face it — the police aren't exactly going to be suspecting one of "their own" could do such a thing, then he'll likely be the first person granted custody of me. There's no way that's happening; I'll live on the streets of Toronto before living with him again.

"Let's make a deal. Give it one more day of searching," Jermaine says. "And tonight you can stay at mine."

I stare at Jermaine, eyes wide. Did he just ask me to sleep over?

"So you're not alone. And my mum will be there, of course," he quickly adds.

The waitress arrives at that moment and unceremoniously plunks two glasses of Coke onto the table before dashing away.

I think about it. On one hand, I really don't want to spend another night alone in that apartment, even though being around familiar things makes me feel closer to Mom. And I have to admit the idea of staying with Jermaine overnight — even if we weren't going to be sleeping in the same room — was exciting. The downside is that I don't want to get a reputation. Jermaine's not my boyfriend. Not that I'm going to have sex with him. But if it gets around that I stayed the night at his place, that's what everyone will assume. And the last thing I want is to be known as a slut.

"Won't your mom mind?" I ask, bending over to take a sip of my Coke.

"She won't think it's safe for you to be going into that empty flat every night. You never know who might be watching and noticing that there's no adult living there right now."

I swallow the Coke, the bubbles burning the back of my throat. What Jermaine says makes sense: I haven't been thinking enough about my personal safety these past few days. My whole focus has been on finding Mom. But if Dad is involved in this somehow, then he's likely looking for me as well.

"Thanks," I say. "You know, not just for inviting me to stay at your place but ... for everything." I pause for a moment, wanting to choose my words carefully. "It was really hard to leave Toronto and Canada and all my friends and stuff. And then Mom ..." I trail off, tears blurring my vision. I hate being so weak; being all emotional isn't going to help bring Mom back.

"You best thank me," Jermaine says. "Now that I'm an accessory after the fact because you told me about the charity money."

I can't contain my tears any longer. They slide down my cheeks in salty rivulets. Even though I feel like a coward for crying, another part of me is glad to finally let out all the fear and sadness I've been bottling up for so long.

Jermaine looks alarmed. "I'm just taking the piss. After all, I'm helping you spend the money right now, aren't I?"

I begin to laugh and cry at the same time, causing the family at the table next to us to glance over. Our waitress arrives at the table with our pizzas. She looks quizzically at us before setting our plates down.

"I'm fine," I say. I use a napkin to wipe my eyes and then pick up my knife and fork. I start to cut my pizza, trying to act as normal as possible. The little boy at the table next to us is still staring at me. I stick my tongue out at him as I stuff a forkful of pizza into my mouth.

# CHAPTER 25

Jermaine's mom emerges from her bedroom and slowly makes her way, with the help of an ornately carved wooden walking stick, into the living room where I sit, chewing my fingernails nervously.

She looks much older than I expected. Although her movements are slow and deliberate, her eyes dance brightly and she smiles the entire time she's walking toward us. A silk kimono the colour of raspberries clings to her thin frame and long silver earrings dangle from her ears.

Now that I'm actually sitting in Jermaine's home, I begin to doubt the decision to stay. Mom will completely freak out about it when she finds out. I'll be grounded until I'm twenty.

With some difficulty, Jermaine's mom takes a seat on the armchair opposite me, carefully tucking her kimono under her. With her high cheekbones and delicate features, she must've been very beautiful when she was younger.

"My son tells me you haven't seen your mother in days," she says. Her voice is gentle but firm.

I look over at Jermaine. Finding out he's told his mother about my secret doesn't sit well with me, though she does seem genuinely concerned.

I nod. "She didn't come home after her first night of work. We only just moved to London and she doesn't really know anyone here. Neither do I."

His mom continues to study me carefully. Her gaze isn't interrogative, though, and I feel strangely safe with her. It's a good feeling after the events of the last few days.

"You'll stay here, then. Jermaine tells me the two of you want to see if you can find her tomorrow. If you can't, I will go with you to the police in the evening." She wraps her slender fingers around the head of a leaping gazelle on the walking stick.

I try to swallow past the lump forming in my throat. "Thank you," I say, even though the idea of going to the police still makes me sick with fear.

She smiles at me, but the smile doesn't touch the sadness in her eyes. "Just remember, Edie, we are never given a hardship greater than we can bear, but Lord knows sometimes we are handed challenges so great that we feel crushed by the weight of them." Then, using her cane for support, she slowly lifts herself out of the chair.

"Jermaine, go and get some bedding out of the wardrobe in my room and fix yourself a space on the sofa. Edie will stay in your room, so make sure it isn't a tip. Good night." She walks back down the hall and to her room, closing the door behind her.

"Be right back," Jermaine says, following his mom.

I relax into the softness of the sofa's cushions and think about what Jermaine's mom said about challenges. Since the night we left Dad, Mom and I have been a team that couldn't be divided; I've always believed if we weren't together, it would be impossible to go on. But these last few days made me realize I need to be able make it on my own. I don't want to, but may not have a choice.

Jermaine comes back out and unceremoniously drops a pillow and blanket onto the opposite end of the couch from where I'm sitting. Then he plunks himself down beside me, draping his arm casually across the back of the sofa so that it rests just behind my head.

"I told you she wouldn't mind you being here," he says, leaning forward to grab the remote control from the coffee table in front of us. In doing so, his arm brushes against my stomach.

"She's great," I say. A siren wails outside the window, its high-pitched squeal momentarily drowning out our conversation and the sound of the BBC news reporter on the television. Scenes of families wading their way through waist-high waters, carrying all their worldly possessions on their backs, flash across the screen, making me feel guilty about the charity money again.

"Too bad you didn't meet her before she got

sick," Jermaine replies. "She was so strong and wouldn't take anything from anyone and let them know it."

I shrug. "Being strong isn't always about being up in someone's face," I say. "Your mom seems pretty strong to me. Look at people like Precious. She's always in my face, but I don't think she'd be all that without her friends backing her every move. Not that running away works either." I pause, not really sure where I'm going with this. "I just wish Mom hadn't run that night. I think we should've tried to fight what Dad was doing."

"Running was probably the safest thing for your mum to do at the time."

"I guess," I say. "But for some reason, he just won't let Mom go. Or me. It's stupid — other people's parents get divorced, remarry, and sometimes even spend holidays together. Why can't he just let us get on with our lives?"

I look over at Jermaine. He's staring intently at me. For a moment, we remain like that, our faces only inches apart. Then he slowly leans in and I feel his breath on my cheek. Then we're kissing. Kissing Jermaine makes me feel both nervous and excited all at once. I can't help but wonder what he's thinking. Does he think I kiss okay or that it's horrible? I wish I'd had the chance to brush my teeth or at least chew gum before this.

His hands wander to my breasts and I push him away.

"Your mom," I whisper. "What if she comes out?"

Jermaine smiles at me lopsidedly. To my relief, he looks as flustered and nervous as I feel.

"My room is next to the toilet. Let me know if there is anything you need," he says, pointing toward the first closed door down the hallway.

"I'm not having sex with you," I say. "Not with your Mom being home." I don't want to tell him I'm a virgin, that being at thirteen different schools has left me with hardly any sexual experience.

"I actually thought we should get some sleep 'cos of tomorrow," he says.

"Oh," I mumble, feeling ridiculous. I get up and subconsciously smooth the front of my jeans. "See you tomorrow."

"Good night, Edie," he says.

Mom's back! I'm standing on the cement platform near the *Cutty Sark* when I spot her. Even though her back is to me and the sun is so bright and warm that it makes me squint, I can tell straight away that it's her. She's wearing her favourite red dress, the one with tiny black, embroidered flowers edging the hem, her hair hanging loose down her back.

"Mom!" I shout. My heart hammers inside my rib cage. Everything's going to be okay now. I hold my hand above my eyes to shield them from the sun's rays. This is by far the warmest it's been since we arrived in London.

She turns and smiles at me. The crazy thing is,

when she turns toward me, I can smell her perfume even though she's standing at least twenty feet away from me. Since I was little, she's always worn this scent that is a mix of vanilla and hibiscus flowers. The smell wraps itself around me like a blanket.

I start to walk, then run to her. But instead of coming toward me, she turns and walks toward a little dome-topped brick building leading to the foot tunnel that connects Greenwich to the Isle of Dogs and the Docklands on the other side of the murky river.

"Mom! Wait for me!" I yell, propelling myself forward.

The thing is, the harder and faster I run, the farther away from Mom I seem to be. She walks through the doorway of the building. In a moment I won't be able to see her anymore. I'm trying so hard to reach her that it's becoming difficult to breathe.

Why is she walking away?

"Mom!" I scream, the effort making the muscles in my throat scream with pain.

But she doesn't turn or even acknowledge me. I throw myself forward, tears streaming down my face.

"Don't leave me! Wait! Don't leave me again!"

A final flash of red and she's gone. I collapse into a heap on the pavement, burying my head in my hands. Great heaving sobs wrack my body. I'm in the exact same spot I was when I first saw Mom. I haven't moved.

I bolt up. Darkness surrounds me like a glove. As my eyes slowly adjust, I make out the shadowy shape of a small dresser against the opposite wall that's illuminated by the moonlight streaming in from a solitary window. A poster of a soccer player named Rooney is tacked above it. Then I remember: I'm at Jermaine's place.

I lie back on the damp pillow and gaze out the window. A sliver of moon peeks through the haze of the sky. All I can do is hope that somewhere out there, Mom is looking up at the same moon.

# CHAPTER 26

"You look tired," Jermaine says between bites of buttered toast and jam.

"Gee, thanks," I mutter, not looking up from my toast. My stomach rumbles hungrily, but just the thought of using energy to chew the bread makes me feel even more exhausted. I put my face in my hands, trying to block out the bright sunshine streaming in through the kitchen windows.

"You mad at me?" Jermaine asks.

I lift my head. "No. Why would I be?"

The silence between us is suddenly electric. My face tingles as I remember last night. "I just had some bad dreams about Mom and didn't sleep that good."

"Well, we're searching today, right?" Jermaine says. "Still have that photo?"

I nod. "But it didn't help much yesterday."

"That's 'cos we're looking in the wrong places! We should go to the hospitals. If your mum hasn't contacted you, it might be because she's got amnesia or is unconscious or something."

I desperately want to believe Jermaine's theory about Mom, but it's too Hollywood. Real life doesn't hand out zany happy endings like that. On the other hand, Mom wouldn't have ID on her with our current address, so there is the tiniest possibility ...

"That's a great idea," I say. "Maybe she's been in an accident or fallen and bumped her head. Or something."

Jermaine looks relieved. "Let's go then," he says.

After eating, we quickly get ready. Having not changed for twenty-four hours, I tell Jermaine I want to stop by the apartment and put on some fresh clothes. Now that I know he might actually like me, the last thing I want is to mess it up by stinking like a garbage can. Our new plan has renewed my optimism, and, as we walk along in the bright morning sunshine, I find myself wondering if the dream last night might've been some sort of sign that Mom was alive and well. I can barely contain my excitement. Why didn't we think to check the hospitals yesterday?

"I reckon we should go to London Bridge first and check out Guy's Hospital," Jermaine says. "It's huge. And it's where I was born, so it's gotta be lucky."

"You wish," I say with a laugh. I look up at the sky. Already the sun is surrendering to an army of grey clouds.

We're nearly at the entrance to the car park in front of our block of flats when Jermaine grabs my hand and yanks me down to the ground.

"What the —" I splutter.

"Shhh," Jermaine says, holding a finger to his lips like I have no clue what the word means. I glare at him.

Ignoring me, he scurries onto a nearby front garden, moving low to the ground with his legs bent like a crab. He waves me over to where he's squatting behind an overgrown hedge.

Something's wrong. I have no idea what Jermaine saw or if what he's doing, but I run over as quickly as I can and crouch down beside him.

"They're there again," he says, keeping his voice low. He straightens a bit and pulls apart a section of the hedge. "Look."

I peer through the bushes, trying to not to poke out my eyes on any of the random branches. The area outside our apartment is empty.

"Second-row walkway," Jermaine says. "Looks like they're knocking on doors and asking the neighbours something."

I look again and there they are: yellow-vested, talking to the neighbours who live directly below us. It looks like it could be the man and woman from last time, but from this distance I can't be one hundred percent sure.

"Maybe they're here for some other reason," I say.

Jermaine looks at me. "You want to take that chance?"

I shake my head. Clearly I'm not going to get a change of underwear and the chance to use deodorant today.

We board a train at New Cross Gate Station. I take the window seat, still nervous that the community officers will find us. I might be slightly paranoid, but considering the life I've led with Dad hunting us down all the time, it isn't surprising.

Within five minutes an announcement informing us that the train is approaching London Bridge breaks the silence of our ride. Butterflies of anticipation dance inside my stomach.

"This is us then," Jermaine says, getting up from his seat.

I follow him into the aisle. Maybe it's because it was a Sunday, but the train seems less crowded, with only a smattering of young families and tourists making their way into the city.

The platform outside the train is more chaotic. Jermaine punches the open button as soon as it lights up and we jump out onto the concrete, nearly falling over a harried-looking mother who's simultaneously battling her young, teary son and hyperactive dog. Both the boy and the dog appear to have decided they aren't going to enter the train without a fight.

The dog, whose wiry grey hair makes it look a lot like a barking toilet brush, wraps its leash around the woman's ankles as the young boy chases it. As the woman bends down in a desperate attempt to try and untangle herself, I catch a glimpse of something directly behind the commotion that makes my heart stop.

My dad is standing there.

Even though it's been a few years, there's no doubt it's him: same spiky black hair (though now receding slightly), same prominent nose that I luckily didn't inherit, and the same strong, sharp jawline.

He's looking at the arrivals and departures screen.

"We need to get out of here," I say to Jermaine. I turn back toward the train, hoping to hop back on before the doors slide shut, but it's too late.

"Wait!" the woman shouts. She runs over to the train door, dog and child dragging behind her, and begins hammering her fist against the glass. Loads of people turn to see what the commotion is about, including my father.

And then, just like in the movies, our eyes meet. I'm sure the look of absolute disbelief and shock that washes across his face is mirrored on my own. He begins to move toward me.

"Run!" I scream at Jermaine. I throw myself in the opposite direction of my father, dashing toward one of the staircases further along the platform.

I reach the stairs and leap up them two at a time, praying I won't trip. Jermaine's beside me within moments.

"What is it?" he asks breathlessly. I shake my head. I can't speak; I don't want to take the risk of slowing us down. My lungs feel like they're on fire.

"Edie!" my father shouts from behind us. He isn't that far behind.

Jermaine is outpacing me now; his long legs allow him to run much faster. We're on the upper platforms now, having to weave around suitcase-carrying tourists, elderly people, and hand-holding couples.

"Get out your Travelcard!" Jermaine shouts over his shoulder to me. He's reached the turnstiles and is sliding through.

My Travelcard! I frantically search my pockets.

"Edie! I just want to talk to you!"

Unable to help myself, I look back. My father is only a few feet away and closing in fast. My bladder loosens.

Where is my Travelcard? I check my back pockets. My fingers suddenly feel as large and awkward as sausages. The Travelcard is there. I slide it into the turnstile and run through. Jermaine is still ahead, running past a tiny newspaper stand and out the doors where several black cabs sit idling.

A rambling, double-decker Vauxhall-bound bus thunders past me, leaving a cloud of exhaust fumes in its wake as I exit the station. Jermaine is waiting for me by two bank machines. As soon as I'm within reach, he grabs my hand and begins to run again in earnest. We reach a crosswalk and he pulls me across just as a black cab is turning into the station, its front bumper missing my legs by inches. The driver leans heavily on his horn.

"Sorry, mate!" Jermaine shouts.

I glance back. Dad is behind us, his tie flapping behind his shoulder as he runs.

"He's still following us," I say.

"Who is he?" Jermaine asks. We reach Borough High Street. Motorcycles and cars whizz by.

"My father."

Without warning, Jermaine leaps into the intersection, taking me with him. A car slams on its brakes.

"What are you doing?" I scream. "Trying to get us killed?"

"No time to wait!" Jermaine says breathlessly.

We reach the other side of the road, bound down a set of stone stairs, and across the front courtyard of an ancient-looking church. Several people eating lunch while lounging on the grass turn and stare.

Jermaine heads down a narrow, cobblestone alleyway. It's packed with people. I don't want to turn around, but hope the crowds will make it harder for my father to continue his pursuit.

"In here," Jermaine says, ducking into a dark doorway. Low, horror-movie-type organ music emanates from the building. A sign above the door reads THE CLINK PRISON MUSEUM.

We make our way down a short flight of steps and press our bodies against one of the walls, trying to make ourselves as inconspicuous as possible.

"This place gives me the creeps," I say, reading a sign on the wall near Jermaine's shoulder. "I can't believe they've made a museum for a prison that was used for torture in the twelfth century." I shudder, wishing we'd found a different place to hide out.

"Back to the important stuff, Edie. That was your dad?" Jermaine asks. "Seriously?"

I nod. " It's crazy. But I told you, he has some sort of sixth sense when it comes to Mom and me."

"Do you think he followed us from New Cross?"

I shake my head. "No. He looked too surprised when he spotted me."

A man dressed in a medieval costume made of red velvet with gold trim approaches us. He takes off his hat and scratches at an inflamed pimple near his glistening hairline.

"Are you two coming in or what? Five pound each."

"Naw," Jermaine says. "We just need to hang here for about five minutes. That okay?"

The man shrugs his shoulders. "I don't mind. It's not like I own the place." He turns and trudges back up the stairs.

"You think maybe your dad is here on holiday?"

"No way," I say.

"Think we've lost him?"

"Who knows," I reply. I pause for a moment. Here I am, running away again because of Dad. When will it stop? Will I be running with my own children someday?

"Actually, I want to find him," I say. "Mom is gone and I'm sure he's got something to do with it. I'm tired of letting him terrorize us and control my life. It's time for him to be the hunted." I turn and head up the museum stairs.

Jermaine grabs my shoulders and turns me around. "Edie, are you sure you want to do this?" he asks.

I shake my head. "Of course I don't want to do this. But what choice do I have? I'm done running."

He leans in and kisses me. "Then I'm right beside you. Let's give your dad some payback."

We emerge back out into the narrow laneway.

"I think we should keep moving in the same direction," Jermaine says. "He was pretty close behind us and likely passed us."

We've only taken a few steps when the screaming starts.

# CHAPTER 27

Most people run away from random screaming. Visions of out-of-control gunmen, raging fire, or other kinds of danger usually spring to mind and most people's instinct for self-preservation kicks in. Jermaine, on the other hand, begins running toward the screams. I don't know what he's thinking, but I follow him anyway, not wanting to be left alone.

We're right by a chicken restaurant when we hear the woman's cries for help. As her shrieks cut through the air like a razor, people sitting outside the restaurant, chicken wings and chicken wraps halfway to their mouths, just sit, kind of frozen.

"What the —" I say, but Jermaine is already running toward an elevated patio filled with umbrella-topped tables. A black metal railing separates the patio from the river. And there, at the railing, a woman stands screaming in despair. A fair-haired toddler in a push-chair beside her begins wailing in unison.

Jermaine is beside the woman in seconds.

"My son!" the woman screams, her arms flailing

crazily in the air above her head. “He’s fallen in! Call 999!”

A couple of people now begin to crowd around. Some pull out phones. I run toward the commotion, thinking we should get out of here. We’ll never find Dad if we get involved.

But before I can reach Jermaine he scrambles over the railing and jumps into the water below. My mouth drops open. What’s he thinking?

I join the others at the railing, including the woman, who is leaning dangerously over, straining to see what’s happening. She’s still screaming, her voice like nails on a chalkboard. Everything seems to be happening in slow motion.

I look over the railing at the murky water below. It laps and whirls hungrily around both of them. Jermaine has the boy, who is as limp as a rag doll, in a loose headlock and is paddling with his other arm toward us.

“Look out!” a deep voice shouts from behind me. A short, square-shouldered man in a white button-down shirt and black trousers pushes past. He’s holding an orange flotation ring in his hands.

“I was just setting up bar in the pub when I heard all the screaming. Took me a minute to realize it wasn’t just some kids messing about,” he says.

“A little boy fell in,” I say. “My friend’s gone after him. They’re right there.” I lean over the railing and point.

“Hang on, lads!” the bartender shouts. “Grab hold of this and I’ll haul you up!” He tosses the orange ring into the water and I can't help but notice how his biceps strain against the cotton of his shirtsleeves.

The ring hits the water with a slapping sound, the wind grabbing it and causing it to land several feet away from Jermaine and the boy. Jermaine paddles slowly toward it. It looks like he's struggling to keep the boy's head above the water now.

Suddenly the boy becomes more alert. His eyes fly open, panic sweeps across his face, and he begins thrashing about, pulling both himself and Jermaine under the water.

The woman begins screaming again. I watch in horror as Jermaine slips under the water. I desperately want to do something. It's such a horrible feeling just standing there, unable to help. First I lose Mom, and now I might lose Jermaine.

Realizing that time is quickly running out, the bartender hurriedly pulls the flotation device back out of the water, tucks it under his arm and slips off his shoes. Then he hops the fence and dives into the water with surprising grace considering his size.

I hear the faint cry of sirens in the distance. Help is on the way, but will it arrive too late? People continue to crowd the railing, watching as the bartender swims toward the spot where Jermaine and the little boy went under.

Suddenly, the crown of Jermaine's head breaks the surface of the water, followed a moment later by the boy's. Both of them are coughing and gasping for breath. Pulling the boy close to his side, Jermaine struggles to stay afloat. The weight of the boy is clearly too much; he looks exhausted.

The bartender tosses the flotation device at Jermaine. It narrowly misses his head and then lands just inches behind him.

"Come on! Grab hold of it, lad!" he shouts.

Jermaine nods weakly. The water is rising around his mouth again. He's sinking.

Nausea sweeps over me. I'm going to vomit.

"Grab it, Jermaine!" I cry. My voice sounds far away, as though I'm screaming down a tunnel.

Jermaine's arm shoots out of the water. He slowly paddles sideways toward the orange ring, which is drifting farther away, pulled by current. The crowd claps in response to his efforts.

The sirens are growing closer, the sound reverberating in my chest.

"You can do it!" the bartender yells as he swims toward Jermaine and the boy.

The encouragement appears to help. Jermaine is suddenly stronger. He reaches the device and tightly grabs hold of it. The crowd begins applauding again, this time the clapping is more frenzied. A woman somewhere behind me begins sobbing.

Fire engines and a white-and-green ambulance pull up alongside the pub. Doors fly open and firefighters and paramedics emerge.

And, as I turn back around, it happens. Jermaine reaches the orange ring and hooks his arm over it so that the crook of his elbow is firmly locked onto the inside of the circle.

"That's the way!" the bartender cries, his voice

cracking with emotion. He begins pulling the rope back, tugging Jermaine and the boy closer to him.

"Clear the way!" a paramedic shouts as he rushes by me. The rescue workers jostle me backward, away from the railing, and into the crowd. There's a flurry of activity. I'm desperate to see what's going on.

Triumphant shouting causes me to push my way through again. Jermaine and the boy are being pulled over the railings by some firefighters. Just the sight of his wet, dark curls makes me start to cry. He looks over, gives me a tired grin and a thumbs-up. One of the paramedics wraps him up in what looks like a huge piece of aluminum foil and sits him down on one of the patio chairs.

The focus of everyone's attention is now on the little boy and his mother, who is near hysterics. A man holds the mother in a tight embrace as she sobs uncontrollably against his chest. The paramedics have the little boy on a stretcher with one of the aluminum foil blankets around him, but they seem to be doing something more. One of the firefighters shouts at the crowd to move back and away.

"Nothing to see. Time to move along," he says.

I catch a glimpse of the little boy and immediately realize something is wrong. His head lolls on his neck like a rag doll's and his face is the colour of campfire ashes. Several firefighters create a barrier with their backs so that the crowd can no longer see what's happening.

"Edie!"

It's Jermaine. He's waving me over. The paramedic attending to him is leading him away toward one of the fire trucks. The bartender is with them. I run over.

"We're taking the little boy to hospital straightaway," the paramedic says. "And I think you two should also go to be checked out. Especially you," he adds, looking at Jermaine. "I know you say you feel fine, but you're a prime candidate for hypothermia and shock."

"I'll go over with him in a cab," the bartender offers. "We've other staff on."

The paramedic smiles gratefully at the man and I wonder if Jermaine is being difficult about the whole hospital thing. "No can do. We'll take you in the other ambulance," the paramedic says. "You know, legalities." He turns to me. "Are you together?"

I nod. "Yes."

"Then we're off," he says.

As we get into the ambulance, I look back toward the little boy. I can just catch a glimpse of him. He's so still and pale, he looks like one of the little plastic action figures I used to play with as a kid. Shivering, I divert my gaze over the river. Under the grey winter sky, the dome of St. Paul's Cathedral sits elevated like a stern old man in the middle of newer buildings surrounding it.

I wonder if Dad is still out there looking for me.

# CHAPTER 28

"James, by the way," the bartender says. He takes a seat opposite us in the back of the ambulance.

"I'm Edie," I say.

"Jermaine," Jermaine says. "Thanks. You know, for everything back there."

"No need to thank me. Though I really did think we were going to lose you a couple of times," James replies. He locks his hands together behind his head and leans back against the wall of the van. "What you did for that little boy today was extraordinary. I hope he's going to be okay."

Jermaine shrugs his shoulders and looks out the back window. "Wasn't anything, really." He pauses for a moment. "But I hope he's okay, too."

"What do you mean it wasn't anything? Didn't you see all those other tossers just standing around doing absolutely nothing? You're a hero. People should know about what you did."

Jermaine arches an eyebrow at James. "No one needs to know."

I can't be sure, but Jermaine's reply seems to make James nervous. He starts rubbing his hands together. Silence fills the van. I agree with James; what Jermaine did back there was nothing short of amazing.

I look out the window and immediately feel ill. Motion sickness is something I've suffered with on and off since I was a little kid and watching London's streets whizzing backwards away from us is too much. Everything outside the ambulance looks washed-out and grey. It's as if the entire city has been put into a washer and dryer too many times, fading all its vibrant colours.

The ambulance slows and comes to a stop outside the hospital's entrance. We hop out and stand waiting for the paramedic, not sure what we we're supposed to do next. Fat drops of rain begin to fall, creating a polka-dot pattern on the concrete at my feet.

"You okay?" I ask Jermaine.

He nods. "Just a bit tired. What happened back there is starting to sink in."

"Here we are," James interrupts. "Tallest hospital in Europe, Guy's is." He motions toward the building with a wave of his hand.

I look up and stared at the gloomy brown building. Hopefully someone put more effort into making the inside more cheerful.

"Has to be the ugliest as well," Jermaine

mumbles, as though having read my mind. I smile at him.

Once inside, James goes to make a quick phone call while Jermaine and I register with the paramedic at the front desk.

"Have a seat," the receptionist says after taking our information. She shoos us toward some uncomfortable-looking plastic chairs with a dismissive wave. Over a dozen other people are already waiting. A bald, middle-aged man sits and moans softly, clutching his stomach, which hangs over the waistband of his pants like an over-inflated beach ball.

"This should be fun," Jermaine says, his voice thick with sarcasm.

James comes back and rejoins us. He seems much quieter, picking up a tattered section of newspaper from one of the empty chairs beside him to read rather than engaging in conversation. Maybe everything that happened earlier is beginning to sink in for him as well.

I sit back and aimlessly watch scenes from a car bombing somewhere in a Middle Eastern country flash across the screen of a bulky television set that is bolted to the waiting-room wall. The camera pans over to a sweaty reporter standing in front of a crowd of angry young men.

"Excuse me, is your name Jermaine? Are you the boy who was involved in the rescue at Bankside today?"

I look up, startled, as a bright light is suddenly

shone on Jermaine. Two men are standing in front of us. The one holding a microphone in Jermaine's face is well-dressed with short, spiky hair and speaks with a clipped accent. Standing beside him is a burly man balancing a television camera on his shoulder.

Jermaine swings around to face James. "What the bloody hell is all this?" he asks. "Is this why you were so desperate to make a call when we first came in?"

James looks taken aback. "What you did was brilliant. God knows we need more feel-good stories in London. Would you rather the news was only filled with images of war and little old ladies being mugged for their pension cheques?"

The reporter nods at the cameraman. The bright light now shines on him, revealing a mask of caked-on makeup, which cracks and creases as he broadens his grin for the camera.

"Hello, London! Welcome to the ITD evening news. I'm Trevor Watson here at Guy's Hospital with the capital's newest hero," he says. "That's right, in this day and age of Asbos and endless stories of hoodie-wearing youths terrorizing our streets, we bring you a good news story about the city's youth."

Every eye in the room is now on Jermaine. Even the bald man has stopped moaning and is intently watching.

The reporter swings around and sticks the microphone in Jermaine's face again.

"Can you tell us exactly what happened in the moments leading up to your daring rescue of that young boy in the Thames at Bankside today, Jermaine …?" the reporter asks.

"Lewis," Jermaine says, finishing the reporter's sentence for him.

"Lewis. Right." A flicker of annoyance momentarily crosses the reporter's face. Then his blinding white smile is back. "So, Jermaine, I think it's fair to say that your Sunday was more than a little out of the ordinary. Wouldn't you agree?"

The camera pans to Jermaine and zooms in for a close-up. He shrugs. "Yeah, I suppose …"

"Can you tell our viewers how you ended up diving into the River Thames this morning, risking your own life to selflessly save that of someone else?" the reporter asks, his face a mask of contrived concern.

"The kid was playing around and fell into the water," Jermaine says. "We heard his mum screaming. I'd have been a twat not to try to save him."

The reporter frowns at Jermaine's use of the word *twat*, which makes me smile. That's what you get for filming this live.

"Do you believe the mother was negligent in allowing her son to play, unsupervised, so close to the water's edge?"

"What?" Jermaine asks. "No, of course not. The kid just fell in. Accidents happen." His face suddenly looks sad. I wonder if he's thinking about what happened to his brother and their friends.

The reporter turns his attention to me.

"And you were with Jermaine when all of this happened? What were your thoughts when you saw him jump in the water to rescue the boy?"

I sit silent for a moment, unable to speak. The light from the camera makes me squint.

"We were looking for my mom," I say. I pause, feeling Jermaine's eyes on me.

"What are you doing?" he whispers, leaning over to me.

"It's okay," I say. "I want to do this. I need to."

I look back at the camera, my eyes adjusting to the brightness. "She's been missing for four days now," I continue, reaching into my pocket and pulling out the photograph. The cameraman zooms in on it. "Her name is Sydney Fraser. I don't know where she is and I'm ..." my voice cracks. "I'm so worried."

The reporter leans in closer. "So, you're telling us your mother has disappeared somewhere on the streets of London?"

I nod. "She was last seen in Camden."

Turning back to the camera, the reporter shares this new bit of news. I hate the way he seems so eager.

"You've heard this breaking news first here on ITD. Sydney Fraser, a Caucasian woman in her ..."

"She's forty-nine," I say.

"In her late forties has gone missing. She was last spotted in the London borough of Camden. If anyone has seen this woman, or has any information on her whereabouts, please contact ITD news or the Metropolitan Police."

Jermaine leans over. "There's no turning back now, Edie," he whispers. He sounds worried.

"I know," I reply. "But I can't do this on my own anymore and I need to know what's happened. Even if it's something terrible."

"This is Trevor Watson reporting from Guy's Hospital. Good night, London!" As the light on top of the camera fades, the reporter turns to us. He extends his hand to me. His grin is wider than ever, making the pancake makeup on his face crack in places like an Egyptian mummy.

"Brilliant! That was just brilliant!" he gushes. "Viewers will be absolutely glued to their screens for updates." He turns to the cameraman. "Brilliant for the ratings," he says.

The words are barely out of his mouth when Jermaine's fist slams into the reporter's carefully powdered chin.

# CHAPTER 29

At first glance, English police stations don't seem much different than Canadian ones. According to Jermaine, this police station in Lewisham is the largest in Europe. To me, the worst thing about being stuck in a police station is that it reminds me of visiting Dad at his work when I was younger.

"We're putting a missing person's file out straightaway," says the officer in charge of looking after us. He seems really young for a police officer, his gangly body attempting without success to fit properly into his uniform. He sits down on the bench beside us.

"I'm Officer Murphy, by the way," he says. "Do you two want anything to drink whilst you wait? It might take a bit of time."

"I'm okay," I reply.

"We're just trying to contact your aunt right now," Officer Murphy says. He looks over at Jermaine. "And your mum."

"Brilliant," he mumbles. "She's going to beat me into next year."

Officer Murphy nods. The expression on his face becomes very serious. "By the way, that reporter isn't going to press assault charges. Apparently that bloke James that you were with somehow convinced him that you were suffering from post-traumatic shock."

Jermaine smiles. "He deserved what he got. He was a wanker."

Officer Murphy shakes his head. "You're just lucky he believed that rubbish. Next time, keep your fists to yourself. No use getting yourself in loads of trouble. If I went punching every twat and idiot I encounter in this city on a daily basis, I'd have fists as raw as mince." He gets up. "Now, if you'll excuse me, I'll check and see what's going on as far as your aunt is concerned."

"Where's your auntie?" Jermaine asks as soon as Officer Murphy walked away. "You didn't tell me you had family here."

"She's not here," I say. "She's somewhere in Ireland. Dublin, I think. I haven't seen her in ages and didn't have any way of contacting her."

"That's tough," he says. "Sorry we didn't find your mum ... or catch your dad."

"That's okay. You saved a kid instead. Not really a wasted day when you look at it that way."

Jermaine smiles. "Can you imagine the look on Ms. Bryans's face when she hears the news?"

I laugh. "Maybe you'll get awarded a medal

from the Queen for bravery and can invite her to the ceremony. She'd die."

"Yeah," he says with a wry smile. "She probably would die 'cos she's so convinced I'm heading for nothing but a life of crime. I'm not inviting that bitch anywhere." He pauses for a moment. "Listen, Edie … you don't really know what's going to happen when they contact your aunt. Where you'll be, you know. Stuff like that."

"I know," I say. "But that's just the way it is. I'm just so tired. All I want is a normal life … to live in one place and go to one school."

"Even if that means being stuck living in Lewisham?"

I turn to Jermaine. "Yep. I'd be especially happy to stay here." And then, without warning, I lean over and hug him close.

Next thing I know, Officer Murphy is clearing his throat uncomfortably. I look up; he's standing in front of us, holding two Cokes. He raises his eyebrows at us, but there's more than a hint of amusement in his eyes.

"Thought I'd bring these just in case you changed your mind about having something to drink," he says. "Jermaine, turns out your mum already learned about your heroics from the telly and is well chuffed. I don't think she needs to find out what happened afterward with the reporter. Unless you want to tell her."

"Really?" Jermaine says, taking one of the Cokes from Officer Murphy. He pulls back the silver tab.

"Thanks, mate. I appreciate it. She has enough on her plate already."

"We'll be taking you home, then," Officer Murphy says. "And let this be the last time you take a ride in a police car, unless you're driving one."

"I'm not becoming part of the police," Jermaine says with a scowl. He turns to me. "I can stay and wait with you if you want. I'll ring my mum. Or you can come and stay at our flat again."

"Actually," Officer Murphy interjects, "we've contacted Edie's aunt and she's booked on an early-morning flight from Dublin." He turns to me. "In the meantime, we've arranged for you to stay with a local foster family tonight."

My entire body goes cold. "But I can stay at my own place," I protest.

Officer Murphy shakes his head. "You know I can't allow that. This is a really nice family and they're just down the road in Greenwich. Jenny and Bill Gilmore. You'll like them. And it's only for one night."

I nod, trying to fight back tears. Part of me wants to just give up, but I know that's not what Mom would want.

"Listen, we'll drive Jermaine home and then take you into Greenwich. It's the best I can do."

I nod again, not trusting myself to speak. Jermaine stands up first. He extends his hand to me and I gratefully take it. Together we follow Officer Murphy and his partner, a female police officer with hair the colour of fire, to the parking lot.

Once outside, the night air strikes me like a slap. It's the coldest night since my arrival. That seems fitting somehow.

Officer Murphy opens the door for me and I slip into the small car. Like everything in London, even police cars are miniaturized. I sigh into the darkness.

Jermaine climbs in beside me. As we drive out of the parking lot and onto a worn-looking residential street that's dimly lit by yellow sodium lights, I realize I have nothing with me.

"I haven't got a toothbrush or pajamas," I say to no one in particular.

"Don't worry. Jenny and Bill will have all the necessities in terms of toiletries and whatnot," Officer Murphy says, not taking his eyes off the road as he navigates the cruiser around a busy roundabout.

I stare out the window at the commuters emerging from the train station. A mother with two young children clutching her hands walks past. I hope they realize how lucky they are.

I close my eyes. Sure, these people will have a toothbrush and pajamas and everything else for me, I think. But they won't be my things. This is it. I'm officially in care, the one thing Mom worked so hard to keep from happening.

The rest of the ride to Jermaine's place is silent. I stare out the window as we drive past a variety of pubs, kebab shops, and Caribbean food shops. Nothing feels real.

Finally, we pull up in front of Jermaine's apartment block. Officer Murphy stops the car, turns on the light inside its cab, and twists around to face Jermaine.

"What you did today was incredibly brave," he says. "That little boy is alive tonight because of you. However, if I ever hear of you doing something stupid like what you did at the hospital, I'll be your personal albatross. Got that?"

Jermaine nods. "Yeah, I got that."

I continue staring out the window. This is it.

"You got a pen and paper, Officer Murphy?" Jermaine asks.

Officer Murphy digs around the glove compartment of the cruiser for a moment and then hands Jermaine a small notepad and a pen.

"Catchy," Jermaine says. I have no idea what he's talking about.

"Don't be cheeky," Officer Murphy replies.

After a few moments of hasty writing, Jermaine folds the piece of paper into a tiny square and hands it to me. I slip it into my coat pocket without looking. Tears blur my vision.

Jermaine leans across the seat. "You don't have to read it now," he says. "Keep your chin up, Edie."

I don't reply; I can't speak. I just want all the hurt to stop and the only way I know how to make that happen is to retreat into myself like a turtle drawing into its shell.

"Thanks for everything, Officer Murphy," Jermaine says as he opens the door and climbs out. The door shuts behind him and I turn away, not wanting to watch him walk to the front door of his building. I can picture it in my head anyhow; I know his saunter, the way he walks with his shoulders out first, swinging one and then the other forward.

I'm so tired of saying goodbye to all the people and things I care about in my life.

## CHAPTER 30

The Gilmores aren't as bad as I thought they'd be. They're actually much younger than I expected, likely in their mid-thirties with no children of their own. Probably taking care of screwed-up kids like me turned them off that idea.

Their house is a narrow, red-brick place on a quiet, residential street. The inside feels warm and safe as soon as I walk into the front hall with its over-filled coat-rack and bright paintings of flowers.

"This will be your room," Jenny says. She opens the door to a cozy room filled with stuffed animals and books. "You can move the toys off the bed, of course," she says with an apologetic smile. "We sometimes get much younger children staying."

I nod. Jenny, with her short, bleached-blond hair and pierced nose, bears an uncanny resemblance to Gwen Stefani. I can hear murmurs of conversation drifting up from the living room below where Officer Murphy and his partner are no doubt filling Bill in on my situation.

"This must be hard for you," Jenny adds. "And you might not want to talk, which is fine. But if you need anything at all, including someone to just listen, let me know. Okay?"

I nod again. Suddenly, a flash of orange and white dashes between my legs and lands like a projectile on the green-and white-flowered bedspread.

"Bedlam! You bloody mad cat!" Jenny cries. She turns to me. "You're not allergic, are you?"

"No, I love cats," I quickly answer. Jenny strides over to the bed and scoops up the cat. It peers excitedly out from under her arm at me.

"Good!" Jenny says. "Because when Bedlam isn't acting like a complete nutter, he's actually quite good company."

I watch as Bedlam begins to struggle against Jenny's arms, kicking with his back feet and wiggling his body in about ten different directions at once in a bid for freedom.

"You can leave him in here," I say. "I hope you don't mind but I think I am going to just go to bed. I'm really tired after everything that happened today."

Jenny frowns slightly. "That's not a problem. Are you sure you don't want anything to eat? We've just finished eating and there's still loads left. And Bill's Spaghetti Bolognese is really something else."

I shake my head. "No thanks," I say. I just want to sleep and escape reality for a few hours.

Officer Murphy appears in the doorway. "Sorry, Edie, but we need to make our way back to the station."

"Thanks for everything," I say.

"My pleasure. I wish things could've worked out differently for you. Here's my card," he says. "Don't hesitate if you need anything."

"Okay," I say. He gives me a little half-wave, turns, and is gone.

I'm overwhelmed by the kindness that so many people — virtual strangers — are showing me. I have no idea what my future might hold now. Maybe Aunt Siobhan won't even want me. After all, as far as I know, she's single and quite a few years younger than Mom. I'm sure suddenly having to take care of a teenager isn't number one on her wish list.

"There are pajamas and toiletries in the top drawer of the dresser for you," Jenny says, interrupting my thoughts. "I'll leave you to it, then."

"Thanks," I say.

Jenny smiles warmly. "You're most welcome. Good night, Edie." She looks at Bedlam, who is kicking at one of the stuffed animals on the bed. "Be good, Bedlam," she says, wagging a finger in his direction. "Just toss him out in the hallway if he bothers you," she adds, closing the door behind as she leaves.

I wake the next morning to the sound of knocking at the bedroom door. Bright sunshine streams into the room through translucent white curtains. I lift my head from the pillow and glance over at the alarm clock on the dresser. It's already eleven o'clock! I've slept for ages.

"Come in," I mumble. I notice the door is slightly ajar and that Bedlam is nowhere in sight.

Jenny peers cautiously into the room. "Good morning, Edie," she says brightly. "I suspected you might want a bit of a lie-in so we didn't wake you, but there is someone here to see you."

I open my mouth to protest. After all, I'm sitting here, hair a mess, teeth unbrushed, wearing some crazy striped flannel pajama set.

But before I have the chance to say anything, Jenny steps aside and another woman walks cautiously into the room. She gives me a nervous smile.

Aunt Siobhan! Though it's been years since I've seen her, she looks nearly the same, aside from her face being thinner than I remember. Same auburn hair, same lopsided smile. She's wearing a simple green shift dressed paired with black motorcycle boots.

"Edie," she says. "Do you remember me? You were so young last time I saw you." Her voice cracks with emotion.

I remember. It was right before everything happened. Siobhan had come to visit us in Toronto. We'd gone all over the city and the entire time Dad was on his best behaviour. He could be so charming when he needed to be.

"Of course," I say. My heart aches. I can see Mom in her eyes, in the way she walks.

She rushes over, sits down, and scoops me up in her arms. I crumple against her. "I'm so sorry all of this has happened to you."

"It's okay," I say just before I burst into tears.

She holds me for a couple of minutes while I sob like a baby.

"What's going to happen?" I ask when I'm finally able to regain composure.

Siobhan lets go of me and takes a deep breath. Her eyes are red and swollen as well. Clearly she's done her own share of crying recently.

"We're going to go by the flat and get some of your belongings," she says. "Edie, the police are there at the moment, so we really need to go as soon as possible."

"Why are they there? What's going to happen to Mom's stuff?"

Siobhan pauses. "The flat is being treated as a crime scene. It seems that some of your neighbours saw Sydney — your mum — struggling with a man a few days ago. The police said they sent people around to try to locate you."

So that's why the community officers were at the flat. If only I hadn't run. Maybe I could've helped them find Mom.

"I've rented us a hotel room not far from here," Siobhan continues. "The police are going to need you to give some statements."

I play with the edge of the bedcover. "Why do they need to talk to me?"

"Your dad came forward to the police today. Apparently the newscast with you and Jermaine compelled him. He's saying that he and your mom were just going to talk, to put closure to things and that she became irate and tried to attack him and, that in defending himself, there was an accident … and she hit her head." She stops and bites her bottom lip nervously. "He took her to his hotel room instead of the hospital. She was unconscious and he was scared. Or so he says. The cause of death was internal brain bleeding. She never woke up, Edie."

The bedcover is fraying. It's coming apart. I continue picking at the threads with my fingers. The world is white noise and I am suddenly very small.

"I wish Sydney had never met him! I'm sorry for saying that, Edie, because you wouldn't be here. It's just she'd still be alive and I would've been able to spend so much more time these past few years with her. She always worried this would happen and that you'd be left alone." Her face twists with pain and sorrow. "She told me everything in her letters. It's all documented and I kept every last one." She begins to tremble and tears slip down her cheeks. "And here I'm supposed to be strong for you."

She hugs me close to her again but I'm numb. All I wanted was the truth but I hadn't really believed I would lose Mom. He found us and I hadn't been able to protect her. We'd come all this way for nothing.

# CHAPTER 31

The Gilmores are giving us a ride to the hotel. Even though they offered to have Aunt Siobhan and me stay a few more nights, I think they're secretly happy to see us go. I don't blame them. Mom's death is making the news already. I found this out by accident when I turned on the television this morning while getting dressed.

I can tell Jenny and Bill feel really bad for me. They were both really quiet this morning and kept giving me these sympathetic, sad looks. And they made me pack all the toiletries like the toothbrush, the housecoat, and even the pajamas I used last night, even though Siobhan insisted she'd buy me stuff later today.

I stare out the car window as we drive down Greenwich High Street. The houses and shops move past in a blur. We stop at a red light. I watch a group of students in their navy blue blazers and matching skirts gather outside a newsagent's. They're laughing and talking and sharing a cigarette. It suddenly hits me that it's Monday. Everyone will be at school — except me.

But everyone will be talking about me. And what Jermaine did saving that little boy. I wonder what he's doing right now. Is he thinking about me?

Bill turns left into a side street and pulls into a small parking lot.

"Don't worry, Edie," he says. "You're not staying at the Café Rouge."

I stare at him. What's he talking about?

Bill hooks points at the building in front of us. A large red sign looms above it. The gold lettering on the sign reads Café Rouge.

I try to smile at Bill to let him know I get his joke now, but the corners of my mouth don't move. Like every other part of my body, including my heart, they feel numb.

"I don't know how to thank you enough," Sioibhan says. "Both of you have been so good to Edie."

"Please," Jenny says, her eyes brimming with tears. "There's no need to thank us. Ring if you need anything at all. Anything." She glances at me, her eyes full of concern. "The next while is going to be so difficult ..."

We get out and Bill takes my tiny bag and Siobhan's two suitcases out of the trunk of the car. He sets them on the ground and shakes Siobhan's hand. Then he comes over to me and gently places his hand on my shoulder.

"You'll be in our thoughts," he says, pressing something into my hand. I look down. A crumpled twenty-pound note sits in the palm of my hand.

I wonder what it's like for Jenny and Bill to not have any children of their own, yet to always be saying goodbye to kids like me that they open their home and their hearts to. They should have kids; they'd be awesome parents and their kids would be so lucky.

I nod at Bill. I feel like I'm acting in a movie, like all of this is make-believe.

Siobhan and I watch as the Gilmores' red Ford Focus pulls away before turning to head into the hotel.

"Do you want your own room?" Siobhan asks as we approach the desk. "They're quite tiny here."

I shake my head. "No," I say.

"It's okay, Edie. Money's not an issue."

I don't want my own room. The thought of being alone, of not knowing where Siobhan is or if she's safe makes my heart begin to hammer in my chest and my palms get damp with sweat. I feel like I might faint.

"Please," I say. My voice sounds far away. "I don't want to sleep in a room alone."

Siobhan lets go of her suitcases and wraps her arms around me. "Oh god! I didn't even think that you might feel that way," she says. "I'm so sorry. Of course we can share a room."

She's right. The hotel room is closet-like, but I don't care. Not knowing where Aunt Siobhan is would drive me over the edge right now. What if Dad's been released by the police and decides to try and find me? What if he hurts Siobhan like he hurt Mom?

Part of me wants to believe that Dad was just trying to talk to Mom. That maybe he was going to apologize, to explain that he's changed and wanted us back. Except down deep I know that isn't true; Mom wouldn't have fought without a reason. She was strong but gentle. If she fought at all, it was in self-defence.

I unpack the few things I have while Siobhan takes a shower then lie down on the bed and flip through some channels on the TV.

I watch a few minutes of *Big Brother* without really caring what's happening. When Siobhan comes out, she sits down in her fluffy white hotel bathrobe beside me on the bed. She smells of grapefruit and soap. With her hair twisted up in a white towel, she looks even more like Mom. Like Mom did.

"Edie," she says. "We need to go to the police station today. You have to make a statement and they're going to want to ask you about the history of your dad's abuse and things."

"Oh," I reply. This is not something I want to do. "Did they let Dad out on bail?"

Siobhan nods. "Yes. The police told me that someone posted bail for him today and they're letting him out as soon as the bank transfer clears. He's not allowed to leave the country, though."

"So he's here. In London," I say. The feeling of panic is starting again. My chest tightens and I feel like there's not enough air getting into my lungs.

"Edie, your testimony might help get the charges upped to murder. It will be circumstantial, but the history of your father's abuse and continued harassment strongly infers that he had a motive to hurt Sydney."

I let everything sink in. My gut reaction is for us to hide out in this tiny space until I know my father is either safely behind bars or back in Canada. But I'm not going to let him keep me running.

"I want to see him."

Siobhan's eyes widen. "What? No. Edie, you don't really mean that."

"I do. I need to. I want to." I stand up and run a hand through my hair. "I've been running from him since I was like, ten years old. I'm not going to run anymore. And I want him to know that."

The look on Siobhan's face tells me she's not sure about this idea.

"I need to see him," I say before she can speak. "So I can tell him I'm going to make sure the police know what happened to Mom and me before her death. To let him know he won't get away with his lie about this being an accident."

# CHAPTER 32

Siobhan insists I try to eat something before we go to the police station. Even though I'm light-headed and dehydrated, I feel like anything I put into my stomach is just going to get puked right back up. But I agree since she's letting me see Dad.

"Sydney loved this restaurant," she says wistfully. "They opened the first one near where we were living in Wimbledon. Your mum and I were sharing a flat together. It was a little piece of Paris in London, she'd say." Siobhan opens her menu and stares at it hard.

We're silent for a few minutes. I look over my menu as well and decide on a sandwich called a croque monsieur. In Canada, I hated French class so much. Now I wonder if I'll ever get the chance to learn it again. As far as I know, England has only one official language. Maybe I can convince Siobhan to let me go to France on summer exchanges or something.

"We lived in that flat when Sydney met your father," Siobhan suddenly says. Her voice is shaky. "I always wonder what would've happened if we hadn't gone to that club the night they met."

I watch her wipe her tears away with the white cloth napkin. "I'm sorry, Edie. I'm probably just upsetting you even more. I'll stop." She takes a deep breath.

"It's okay," I say. And it is. I suddenly realize I haven't shed a tear since initially finding out Mom was dead.

Eating lunch doesn't go very well for either Siobhan or me. She downs three espressos in about a minute and then eats about four bites of salad before giving up.

I tear at the crust of my sandwich and watch several mothers with young children trying to have lunch at the table beside us. It seems like every few seconds there's a kid screaming, running away, or attempting to turn his or her food into a projectile. The women all look like they've gotten dressed in the dark and forgot to brush their hair. Still, they've got their kids, and their kids have them.

The sandwich tastes like sawdust in my mouth. Chewing makes my jaw ache and I only manage a couple of bites. I'm worried if we don't get to the station soon, Dad will be released.

The drive seems to take forever. Neither of us says much. It's hard to believe that just yesterday I was here, still hoping Mom was alive and that everything would turn out okay.

Officer Murphy is on duty. He comes right over.

"I'm so sorry about your mum, Edie," he says.

He looks like he's about to cry. I feel like I should say something to comfort him, which is stupid because I'm the one with the completely screwed-up life.

He clears his throat and turns to Siobhan. "Officer Murphy," he says, shaking her hand. "You must be her aunt. It's wonderful that you've made it here so quickly. I'll be the one taking Edie's statement."

"I want to see my dad," I say.

Officer Murphy's eyes widen with surprise. "I don't think we can do that."

"Find out. Please," I add.

He looks at Siobhan. "We'd need your consent as your acting in the parental role …"

Siobhan pauses for a moment. "I don't think this is a good idea, but Edie feels this is something she needs to do. Only she knows what will bring her closure and I need to respect that."

Officer Murphy looks at me. "It's not as easy as you think, Edie. A team would need to do an assessment for risk, evaluate your emotional well-being, and then determine if such a visit is in your best interest. Given the close proximity to your mother's death, I highly doubt the visit would be granted."

"But I'm fifteen," I protest. "I'm old enough to know if something is going to make me emo or not. I need to see him."

The doors bursts open and two officers, one female and one male, come in, both of them struggling to contain this guy with grey, ropey hair who looks like he hasn't bathed in years.

"We need backup!" the woman shouts, her face flushed from the effort of trying to keep the man from escaping.

A horrid stench is filling the air around us. The man lifts his head and roars.

"Get off me, you bleeding bastard pigs!" he shouts.

And that's when I recognize him. It's the man from the phone booth. I quickly look away as other officers rush over to help.

"Come with me," Officer Murphy says, taking me by the elbow and leading me away. "You've got all of two minutes, tops." He buzzes us through a side door that takes us into a grey hallway. The metal door closes behind Siobhan with a loud click.

We follow him down the hall. There are several cells on either side. Some are empty and several are occupied by a variety of people, mainly men, who either ignore us, glare at Officer Murphy hatefully, or stare at Siobhan and me with intent.

"Hey, gorgeous," one of them calls as we walk past. I ignore him and keep my mind focused on facing Dad.

Officer Murphy stops in front of a cell and turns to me.

"I could get the sack for this, Edie," he says. "Please make it fast."

I nod and approach the cell, noticing how Siobhan is hanging back, a look of sheer hatred on her face. I think she'd tear Dad apart with her bare hands if she could.

Taking a deep breath, I step in front of the bars. Dad is sitting hunched over on a small bunk, his hands clasped in front of him, his head hanging down. He looks up at me. His eyes glitter with tears. Purple circles frame his eyes.

"Edie," he whispers. "I'm so sorry. It was an accident."

And, for a moment, I feel so sad that my father is locked up in here. The place looks awful, and there is graffiti carved into the walls. I want to hug him and feel his strong arms around me just like when I was little, when I still believed he was the one who would protect me from the monsters under the bed and the ones out in the real world. I can still remember the smell of his aftershave.

Only he turned out to be the monster.

He gets up and walks over. "I love you. I loved your mother. It was an accident.... You have to believe me. She was pushing my buttons."

And that's when something in me snaps.

"You ruined our lives," I say, trying to keep my voice steady. I make myself look him in the eye. "And you took Mom's life away. But you're not going to ruin my life anymore. The police are going to know everything. How you stalked us. How you used to hit Mom all the time and make her bleed. How you fractured her wrist that time and made her tell everyone she fell while jogging."

"Edie," Dad says. "I've changed. That's what I came here for. To let your mother know that."

"If you'd really changed, Mom would still be

here. You'd have left us alone to get on with our lives."

"You're being just like her, too headstrong and emotional. I was trying to calm her down when everything happened," he interjects. There's an edge to his voice that I recognize. I'm making him angry.

"That's right," I say. "I am just like her — not like you. She was strong, loving, and gentle. She protected me every single day of my life. And she paid for that with her life. You need to stay away from me. Forever." I pause for a moment, looking him in the eyes. He looks away first. "And if you come after me, I'm not running," I add.

I take a deep breath, turn and walk back down the hall with Siobhan and Officer Murphy right behind me.

Once we're on the other side of the door again, I collapse into Aunt Siobhan's arms and sob. I cry for at least half an hour until I can't squeeze out any more tears. Mom's gone. I'm never going to see her again. I can't believe I'm not able to just dial her cell number and hear her ask me how my day was. I miss her so much. My chest hurts and my heart feels like it is being torn apart. Everything hurts now.

# CHAPTER 33

That night I tell Aunt Siobhan there are a couple of things I still need to take care of. This is going to be my way of proving to myself, once and for all, that I'm not like my father; that I'm not going to go around hurting people just to get what I want.

The next day I show up at school. From the moment I walk in, things are different. I've gone from being the girl who hardly anyone noticed to being the most recognized person in the place. It's disconcerting having all these people I don't even know coming up to me and expressing condolences about Mom. My gut reaction is to ignore them or tell them to piss off, but I don't want to just think about myself anymore. There's no need to keep living on survival mode.

My first stop is the office. The front desk secretary looks up as I approach.

Pity floods her eyes. I bite my lip and manage a smile.

"Is Mr. Middleton around?" I ask.

"He is, Edie. Would you like to see him?" she asks, taking off her glasses and giving me a sympathetic smile.

"Sure. I mean, yes. Please. It will just take a minute." Impulsively, I finger the wad of bills in the front pocket of my skinny jeans to make sure it hasn't somehow disappeared.

"I'm sure he'd be happy to see you," she says, picking up the phone. "By the way, will we be seeing you soon? It would be grand to have you back here at Windrush."

*As soon as my mother's funeral is done and my father's murder trial is over*, I want to say. After being so careful to conceal our private life all these years, it makes my stomach churn to know that our entire story is everywhere. However, she's being sincere and I need to appreciate the fact that people are concerned about me.

"Not sure," I say. "I'm going to be living with my Aunt Siobhan in Ireland for a little while, I think."

"Well, just know the door is always open here," she says. "Go ahead in." She waves me toward Mr. Middleton's office.

He greets me at the door. He's wearing his usual suit and tie. Today it's a navy check with a red tie. He places his hand on my shoulder. "I hope you realize the entire Windrush community is here for you," he says. "We'd like to hold a little fundraiser for you and your aunt next week. That is, if you feel comfortable with that."

Tears spring to my eyes. "That's really nice of

you," I say. "But … I don't think I deserve it. My aunt might be able to use the money, though. Seeing how she's suddenly inherited me." I try to smile, but my bottom lip begins to tremble uncontrollably, and, instead, I end up with tears spilling down my cheeks.

"Take a seat, Edie." Mr. Middleton pulls a chair in front of his desk for me. "This must be an incredibly hard time for you."

I nod. My nose is beginning to run. Mr. Middleton hands me a tissue.

"Sorry," I mumble.

Mr. Middleton's eyes widen. "You needn't apologize."

He doesn't know how I hate this, how I hate having my emotions out on public display like this. I take a deep breath and compose myself.

"I need to give you something," I say, rummaging around in my pocket and pulling out the wad of bills.

Confusion washes over his face. "I don't understand. Why …"

"I was the one who took the charity money from the class," I say, interrupting Mr. Middleton mid-sentence. "It wasn't Jermaine, though he took the fall for me."

There's no denying the surprise on Mr. Middleton's face. "Why wouldn't Jermaine have said something? He's ended up with another permanent suspension on his record because of this."

"Because he's not a rat. And I think he's kind of given up on expecting people to see him for who he really is. But he's smart, and a really loyal friend,"

I reply, holding the money out to Mr. Middleton. "Anyway, it's all there. The eighty pounds. I don't mind if you want to have a fundraiser so things are easier for Aunt Siobhan, but this money needs to be given to its original cause."

It's noon by the time I leave Mr. Middleton's office, so I head straight for the cafeteria, hoping she'll be there. There's one more thing I need to do.

I'm not disappointed. Scanning the room, I see her, sitting alone, head buried in a book at table in the far corner of the room.

"Hey, is this seat taken?" I ask, plopping myself down on a chair opposite Imogen.

Startled, she looks up at me, eyes wide. "Edie!" she says, pushing her glasses back up the bridge of her nose. She smiles widely for a brief moment, and then remembering, suddenly grows sombre. "I'm so sorry about your mum."

I nod. It's the first condolence today that's really touched me. "Thanks, Imogen," I say.

"How are you doing?" she asks, then immediately shakes her head. "That was so stupid of me. Of course you're not going to be doing well."

I smile at her. "It's okay. I'm actually doing better, thanks. It's hard to get up in the morning, but every day it gets a little bit easier."

"Still, it must be hell," Imogen says, staring hard at her plate of fries. Today's fare is so greasy, the fries practically glisten under the fluorescent lights of the cafeteria.

"Yeah, it is," I admit. "Listen, I came back to school to talk to you." I pause for a moment. "And to return the charity money."

Imogen's mouth drops open. "You took the money?" she asks, incredulously. "I thought Jermaine did."

I shake my head. "Nope. I took the money and let Jermaine take the blame. What a bitch, eh?"

Imogen raises an eyebrow at me. "Kind of," she says. "Especially considering he's the type of person who risks his life for little kids."

We're silent for a few moments.

"I came back because I need to apologize to you," I say. "I treated you really badly when I was around Savitri and Keisha. That was wrong. You were the first person to make me feel welcome here. And you gave me the heads-up about Precious," I add, shooting her a smile. "Seriously, though, Imogen, you're a nice person and what I did was really out of order."

"You're starting to sound more English," she says. "And thanks for the apology, but it's no big deal. I mean, it's not like you're the first person who didn't want me around. I'm kind of used to it." She looks down at the table.

"It is a big deal. People shouldn't treat you like shit. Especially Precious. You're a much better person than her."

"Well, I won't have to worry about her anymore," Imogen says, looking back up at me. "Her mum was arrested for beating her up in the front garden of their flat last week, wasn't she? Precious was taken into care. Everyone in the neighbourhood knows about it. Apparently her mum knocked her two front teeth right out before the police arrived."

I sit back and breathe out heavily. It never occurred to me that other kids might be dealing with domestic violence as well. That definitely explained Precious wanting to lash out at everyone around her. I have to admit to understanding that feeling all too well.

"Are you coming back?" Imogen asks, interrupting my thoughts. "I mean, back here to Windrush? Or will you return to Canada?"

I think about it for a minute. Now that I'm with Aunt Siobhan, I'm going back to Ireland with her. Another place I've never been; another place where I'll be a complete foreigner. At the same time, there's no one left for me in Canada. Not in terms of family, anyhow.

"I'm not sure where I'll be eventually," I reply. "But why don't we stay in touch? Do you have a pen and paper?"

Imogen grins. "Really?" she asks, leaning down and unzipping her knapsack.

"Really," I say as she hands me a pen and her school agenda. "I'm giving you my email address and I expect some communication."

"It's a deal," Imogen says. "Take care of yourself, Edie. Remember your friends are here for you."

I walk over to her and give her a hug before walking away. "I will," I say. "I promise."

## CHAPTER 34

"Thanks," I say as the stewardess hands me a glass full of ice and a miniature can of Diet Coke. I look over at Aunt Siobhan, who is nervously unwrapping a stick of gum.

"Want one?" she asks. "It's the take-offs I can't stand."

I shake my head. "No, thanks," I say. "So, what happens next?"

We've been living in Dublin for the last six months while Siobhan trained someone to take her position so that we could make our permanent move to London. Siobhan also felt it was best for me to be out of England; Mom's murder and Dad's impending trial were all over the media and journalists were constantly snapping photos of us.

Mom's funeral and most of the last few months are a blur for me. It's only now that I'm beginning to feel emotions other than anger and grief again. I still lose it a few times a day, but at least I find myself sometimes thinking about other things or enjoying a television show or movie. It's a start. And I miss being in school.

"Well, we've got a flat set up. Nothing posh, so don't get your hopes up." Siobhan smiles. "But it's nice. I think you'll like it. We've got a little garden and everything."

The engines start up with a roar. The plane begins to taxi down the runway and Siobhan grips at the armrests so tightly the skin over her knuckles whitens.

"It's not near your old school, unfortunately," she says through gritted teeth.

"That's okay," I say. "I've kept in touch with everyone I wanted to from there anyhow." *Especially Jermaine*, I want to add, but decide against it. Aunt Siobhan doesn't need to know that I've already got a date to meet up with Jermaine the day after we arrive back.

"Listen, I've arranged for you to see someone for a while to talk about everything," Siobhan says. "Are you okay with that?"

I slosh the ice cubes around in my drink for a moment, letting them bump against the sides of the plastic cup.

"Yeah," I say. "I'd rather talk than just stuff it all away. I think it's good to talk. If more people talked about things that happen in their homes that no one sees, rather than feeling ashamed, there might be less violence. Maybe Mom would still be here."

I look out the window as we take off into the grey skies over Ireland. I still feel really angry and sad inside, but like the fact that my life is going to become more regular now. Aunt Siobhan has no idea how much I ache to go to the same school day after day.

I reach into my jacket pocket for the photograph of Mom I put in there earlier today. My fingers touch a piece of paper: Jermaine's note. I take it out and unfold it. I've read it and reread it so many times these last few months that it's practically disintegrating along the folds.

*Edie — You're the only person I can truly call a friend. When things get tough, don't forget to lean on those who love you. Jermaine.*

I fold the paper back up, put it in my pocket and lean back into the seat. No matter what awaits me in London, I can face it. No more running. I smile and grab hold of Aunt Siobhan's hand.

# MORE GREAT YA FICTION FROM DUNDURN

THROWAWAY
GIRL

by
kristine scarrow

*So many girls my age can't wait to get out on their own, counting down the days until they leave home, anxious to have their space and a place of their own. But when it comes right down to it and you only have yourself in this world, you don't feel that way.*

***A throwaway girl, that's what I call myself.***

Andy Burton knows a thing or two about survival. Since she was removed from her mother's home and placed in foster care when she was nine, she's had to deal with abuse, hunger, and homelessness. But now that she's eighteen, she's about to leave Haywood House, the group home for girls where she's lived for the past four years, and the closest thing to a real home she's ever known.

Will Andy be able to carve out a better life for herself and find the happiness she is searching for?